Irish author **Abby Green** ended a very glamorous career in film and TV—which really consisted of a lot of standing in the rain outside actors' trailers—to pursue her love of romance. After she'd bombarded Mills & Boon with manuscripts they kindly accepted one, and an author was born. She lives in Dublin, Ireland, and loves any excuse for distraction. Visit abby-green.com or email abbygreenauthor@gmail.com.

# AN INNOCENT, A SEDUCTION, A SECRET

## ABBY GREEN

# MILLS & BOON

First Published in Great Britain 2018
by Mills & Boon, an imprint of HarperCollins*Publishers*
1 London Bridge Street, London, SE1 9GF

© 2018 Abby Green

ISBN: 978-0-263-93506-6

MIX
Paper from
responsible sources
**FSC** **FSC‑ C007454**
www.fsc.org

This book is produced from independently certified FSC™ paper
to ensure responsible forest management.
For more information visit www.harpercollins.co.uk/green.

Printed and bound in Spain
by CPI, Barcelona

This is for Jamie Mulhall,
thanks for your insight into luxe shopping,
displays and dressing! xx

# CHAPTER ONE

'JUST A COUPLE more questions, if I may, Mr Rivas?'

Sebastio Rivas gritted his teeth but forced himself to smile. 'Of course.'

The words of his solicitor and chief advisor rang in his ears.

*I know you hate this, Sebastio, but since your father died a year ago you're now the face of Rivas Bank and everyone wants a piece of you. You're going to have to do a certain amount of letting the media in...and the public. They want to meet the man who has single-handedly turned one of the world's most debt-ridden institutions back into a respected and successful bank.'*

His smile must have been scary, because the journalist from one of the world's leading financial broadsheets was looking at him nervously.

Sebastio's suit felt constricting, his tie too tight. It was at moments like this that he longed most for his past—to be wearing the colours of his country, with fourteen teammates behind him and nothing but the reverent hush of a vast rugby stadium as everyone waited with bated breath to see if he could deliver the ball over the bar.

He missed the simplicity of working with a team with one aim in mind. Winning. Being the best they could be. Coming together in a fluid cohesive unit that was unstoppable. He'd never come across that amazing feeling of solidarity again.

*Because you ruined it.*

The journalist cleared his throat, bringing Sebastio back into the present moment—which was just as well because he had no desire to take a trip down *that* memory lane today.

The journalist apparently couldn't read Sebastio's mind, because he said blithely, 'Your life is very different now from the world you inhabited before—that of a professional athlete playing international rugby for your country. You never showed any interest in banking until a few years ago, and yet your transition has been successful, to say the least. You have returned Rivas Bank to profitability within mere months of your father's death.'

Sebastio's eyes narrowed warningly but the young man stared him down. Maybe he wasn't so nervous after all. Sebastio had to concede that of course there was no way he wasn't going to be asked to explore this avenue. He had been one of the most celebrated athletes of his generation, captaining Argentina against the world's best teams, beating them again and again, ushering in a golden era for Argentinian rugby.

He was very tempted to cut the interview short, but knew he couldn't, so he forced that smile again and said coolly, 'I've always been interested in banking. The Rivas family were one of the first to open a bank in the Americas, so it's been in my blood for many generations.'

'And yet the Rivas bank fell into something of a decline in recent times.'

Sebastio's smile turned even more forced. 'That is true. However, that decline is in the past now.'

Sebastio didn't need to be reminded of what had precipitated that decline. He'd lived it. Witnessed it all too closely.

It had come about for many reasons—the main one being Sebastio's parents' very high-profile and scandalous divorce. Scandalous because of the flagrant infidelities on both sides. And because of the life of excess exposed by the court case. Not to mention the vicious custody battle over eight-year-old Sebastio.

When the dust had settled, and Sebastio's father had been granted primary custody of Sebastio, he'd proceeded to drink and gamble his way through what had been left of the family wealth and profits from the bank.

Admittedly Sebastio hadn't done much to help when, as the only son and heir, he'd turned his back on his inheritance to play rugby professionally—which had had as much to do with rebelling against his family as it had to do with his love of the sport.

Thanks to his glamorous background, good looks and sporting prowess, and his aversion to commitment, he'd developed a reputation as one of the world's most eligible bachelors. And one of the world's most notorious playboys.

When Sebastio had stepped away from the rugby field, however, the bank had convened an emergency meeting, in order to appeal to him to reconsider taking up his position on the board. And once he'd realised how many thousands of lives were supported directly and indirectly through the bank—how many lives his father had been playing roulette with—he'd had no choice but to take his place and regain control of the sinking ship.

He'd already had enough guilt on his conscience to last him a lifetime. He hadn't needed the added guilt of watching thousands of lives decimated, thanks to his father's weaknesses.

He'd spent the last three years assuming more and more responsibility as his father had entered into a decline brought on largely through self-destruction and bitterness.

Hugo Rivas had never really got over the fact that the most beautiful woman in Argentina had wanted to divorce him.

People said of Sebastio's stratospheric success that his innate ability to understand the intricacies of finance and manage a financial institution was genetic, but he considered it merely fortuitous.

The journalist's voice cut into his circling thoughts. 'You walked away from rugby after the tragic car accident involving Victor Sanchez and his wife. How much of a part did the accident play in your move back into the family business? And are you still in touch with Victor Sanchez?'

The question had the effect of a small but devastating bomb inside Sebastio. He had never spoken about the catastrophic accident that had claimed two lives, ruined a third and blighted his own for ever. And he certainly wasn't about to start.

He stood up smoothly, buttoning his jacket as he did so. 'If that's all… I have a meeting to attend.'

The journalist stood up too, with a wry smile, and held out his hand. 'I hope you don't blame me for trying, Mr Rivas. My editor would never forgive me if I didn't ask the question everyone wants answered most.'

Sebastio took the journalist's hand and squeezed it firmly enough to make the man's eyes water slightly. He bared his teeth in another cordial smile. 'You can ask all you want—not that I'll ever answer.'

He turned and walked out, trying to ignore the beat of anger pulsing in his blood that a stranger had opened this Pandora's box of unwelcome memories. Memories of the worst night of his life.

The screeching tangle of metal on metal and the smell of leaking petrol was still vivid enough to make Sebastio break out in a cold sweat. And the image of his friend's wife, thrown from the car and lying at an unnatural angle on the road, blood pooling around her head.

His mouth was a grim line as he pulled on his coat and exited the exclusive hotel in London's Knightsbridge. He was thousands of miles from Buenos Aires and yet the past wouldn't leave him in peace.

*You don't deserve it.*

The line of his mouth got tighter. He *didn't* deserve peace. So maybe he owed the journalist something for reminding him of that.

He saw his driver jump out of his waiting car and rush around to open the door and that feeling of constriction was back. He said, 'It's okay, Nick. I'm going to walk back to the office.'

The suited man inclined his head. 'Very well, sir. Nice day for it.'

*Was* it a nice day for it? Sebastio watched as the driver pulled out smoothly into the snarl of London traffic. He supposed that yes, it was a *nice day*. It was one of those rare English winter days—bright and clear and dry. Frost was in the air, but not on the ground yet. Christmas was around the corner and the decorations were up in earnest.

Sebastio passed women in expensive furs and men in bespoke suits and overcoats, much like his own.

He pulled up his collar against the chill and was oblivious to the appreciative looks he drew from a group of women standing outside a shop. He crossed the street, avoiding a particularly garish Christmas tree surrounded by singers in period costume belting out tuneless carols.

He loathed Christmas for too many reasons to count, and for the past three years had escaped it by going to parts of the world where Christmas wasn't celebrated so much. One year he'd gone to Africa, another year to India. Last year he'd spent it in Bangkok.

That first year—after the accident had happened—Christmas had been a blur of grief, guilt and pain so acute that Sebastio hadn't been sure he would come out the other side.

But he had. And this year he was here in London, in the hub of Christmas mania. Because the truth was that he didn't deserve a free pass to escape. And, more pertinently because the Rivas bank had just opened its European headquarters here. He had been advised to make the most of the festive season by hosting a series of important social functions which would secure his place in English and European society.

It had even been suggested that he should decorate his house, where he was intending hosting these seasonal social functions, but the thought of being surrounded by trees and baubles and blinking lights made him feel so claustrophobic that he'd tuned out that particular advice.

He was passing the windows of one of the most famous department stores in the world now, and an ornate sign hung in the window, in front of red velvet drapes.

*The famous Marrotts festive windows*
*will be revealed this weekend!*
*Happy Christmas!*

A couple of small children were trying to peer in between a small gap in the curtains, giggling before being led away by their parents.

Sebastio felt a shaft of pain so intense that he almost stopped dead in the street. If not for the accident, Victor and Maya's daughter would now be…

He shook his head to dislodge the thought and instinctively moved away from the main thoroughfare, ducking down a side street. He cursed the reporter again for having precipitated this avalanche of memories.

At that moment Sebastio turned his head and realised he was passing another of those famous windows, but this time the red velvet drapes were partially open.

He came to a reluctant standstill on the quiet pavement as the scene in the window snagged his attention. It was a magical fairy forest, with branches opening into hidden worlds and little faces and eyes peeping out. Fairies, goblins...

In spite of himself, Sebastio was momentarily captivated. It was Christmassy, but...*not*. It tugged on a memory deep in the recesses of his mind. An uncomfortable reminder that he hadn't always hated Christmas.

He'd had an English grandmother, and his parents had used to leave Sebastio with her every Christmas while they went on holiday. Those Christmases had been magical. His grandmother had taken him to West End shows. They'd decorated the house, watched movies, played games. All the things he'd never done with his parents because they had been too busy either having affairs, fighting or indulging in lavish reunion holidays.

Sebastio had used to dread their return, and he could remember one year clinging to his grandmother in tears, his father pulling him away roughly...

His grandmother had died not long after that, and they hadn't even come back to England for her funeral. Sometimes Sebastio had wondered if he'd made it up. So starved of affection by his parents that he'd concocted a benevolent loving grandmother like some pathetic fairytale...

As time had passed it had seemed more and more like a fantasy because no subsequent Christmas had ever been like those idyllic ones he remembered. And so he'd blocked them out and convinced himself that he hated Christmas, because he knew he would never experience anything close to that magic again and to want it was a weakness.

He saw movement, and followed it to see a woman standing at one side of the display. She had her hands on her hips and her head cocked to one side as she looked up to where a young man was hanging a glittering star on the branch of a tree. They must still be dressing the window.

She shouldn't have snagged his attention. She had her back to him and she was dressed in plain black trousers, a long-sleeved black top and flat shoes. He saw her shake her head, her shining cap of short hair glinting auburn in the lights. Then she bent down and picked up something else—another decoration—and handed it up to the man on the stepladder. As she reached up, her top rode high to reveal a taut pale belly and slim waist.

A beat of something pulsed to life in Sebastio's blood. Awareness. Arousal. For a moment he almost didn't recognise it, it had been so long since he'd felt it. *Nearly four years.* He welcomed it as an antidote to the bitter memories.

Then, as if sensing his attention on her, the woman slowly turned around. Sebastio wasn't prepared for the kick to his solar plexus when he saw her revealed. She was stunning. Huge eyes framed by arching dark brows. Defined cheekbones and a lush mouth set off dramatically by her short hair, slightly longer at the front and feathering messily around her face.

It gave her a delicate gamine appeal that sent a definite surge of desire through Sebastio's body. It confounded him. Being so tall and big himself, he'd always gravitated towards statuesque women. This one looked as if a puff of wind would blow her over. And yet he could sense an inner strength. Crazy when she was a total stranger, with a thick pane of glass separating them.

The woman was staring at Sebastio with an arrested

expression. For a moment their eyes locked. Hers were deep blue, but even from here he could see the long lashes. And then, as if waking from a trance, she stalked over and dragged the drapes shut, leaving Sebastio looking back at his own distorted features in the glass.

He had the strangest sensation of déjà-vu—as if he had seen her somewhere before. But the feeling was too ephemeral to pin down.

He was stunned. No woman had ignited his interest or his desire so forcibly and immediately in four years. Not that anyone would believe it. Sebastio was a master of misdirection—covering up his flatlining libido with a series of high-profile dates that never went beyond a kiss. His reputation as a skilled lover and a connoisseur of beautiful women served as a smokescreen he used willingly.

He thought of the display in the window again. It had effortlessly captured his attention, taking him unawares, which was unusual when he had such an aversion to Christmas. He thought of the advice he'd been given to decorate his home and something occurred to him...

That woman might have sparked his libido back to life, but he needed her for something far more practical.

Sebastio went back the way he'd come and turned the corner into the main street, thronged with people. He saw the main doors of the shop and strode towards them purposefully.

Edie Munroe was standing looking at the closed drapes like someone who'd been hypnotised. Or hit over the head. She'd never in a million years expected to see that guy again and yet...she just had.

And it had struck her today as forcibly as it had four years ago, when she'd first laid eyes on him in a crowded nightclub in Edinburgh.

*It couldn't be him*, she told herself now, feeling her skin rise into goosebumps. It couldn't be Sebastio Rivas.

The fact that she even remembered his name was not welcome.

What were the chances it *was* him? It had to be someone who looked liked him. After all, Sebastio Rivas was a mega-famous international rugby star. What on earth would he be doing walking down a random side-street in London?

But her accelerated heart-rate told her it *was* him.

It was galling to be reminded that no other man in four years had had the same effect on her. And she'd tried. She'd gone on Tinder dates, blind dates and internet dates. But on each date, when the guy had tried to take things a step further, Edie had felt herself shutting down.

Because she couldn't get out of her head how *he'd* made her feel four years ago. Alive and energised. Buzzing. *Connected*. Hopeful.

And aroused.

For the first time in her life she'd understood what people were talking about when they spoke of *instant attraction*, or said, *You'll know it when you feel it*. She had felt it like a palpable energy. Electricity.

It had been a wholly new sense of desire, and she'd known instinctively that only he could assuage the building sense of excitement in her core. A crazy assertion to have about a total stranger, but one so deep she could still feel it today.

It was pathetic. Her entire exchange with Sebastio Rivas had lasted about five minutes. He'd told her to *run along*. He'd been out of bounds, out of her league, and he hadn't hesitated in letting her know.

The fact that she'd gravitated across a heaving dance-floor to orbit the sun of his smouldering sexuality—like every other woman in the room—was as freshly humiliating today as it had been then, especially after he'd sent her on her way.

She'd been so sure she'd seen something…sensed something in him. Their eyes had locked and a silent communication had throbbed between them. She'd seen something in his demeanour, in his eyes, a kind of brittleness. And it had resonated within her because she'd felt the same.

She'd just come through a major ordeal—cancer, which she'd contracted when she was seventeen, throwing her life into instant turmoil. It had become a fight for survival, an endless round of toxic treatments and sterile hospital rooms.

For the previous eighteen months she hadn't known if she would live or die, and some of the time she'd been feeling so sick she'd almost wished—

Edie clamped down on that thought, remembering her parents' worried, pinched faces.

That very day she'd been given the all-clear, and that night had been her first foray back into the world. She'd felt as if a layer of skin had been removed, making everything feel too bright, too sharp. Too much.

She remembered that she'd been wearing a dress borrowed from a friend. Short, silver and slinky. Not her style at all. But then, that whole night had been about a celebration she'd never expected to experience. A celebration of life.

And, because her hair hadn't yet started to grow back, she'd been wearing a wig. A shoulder-length bob. Bright red and hot and scratchy. Yet none of that had stopped her from approaching the most beautiful man in the room.

She'd never seen or met a man who'd come close to his sheer charisma and good-looks. Well over six foot, he'd had the leanly muscled build of an elite athlete. The power in his body had been evident under his dark suit.

A little desperately, she tried to tell herself again that

the man she'd just seen outside couldn't be him. But she'd never forget that face. Sculpted from stone. All slashing lines and sharp bones. Hard jaw. Deep-set eyes under black brows. Thick dark hair flopping messily over his forehead. Curling around his collar.

And a mouth made for sin. Full and sensual. Softening those hard lines and the stern demeanor he'd exuded like a force-field.

'Edie... Earth to Edie... Can I come down now?'

She whirled around, aghast at her reaction to someone who probably wasn't even the man she was thinking of. She was losing it.

'Of course, Jimmy.' She gabbled, 'I think the man in the window— I mean, the man in the moon decoration works better than the star.' She hoped Jimmy wouldn't see her face flaming at her Freudian slip.

'Not that anyone will see it,' grumbled the young man as he came down the ladder. 'We're all the way around the corner from the main windows.'

Edie said brightly, 'It means we can be more creative with our wee display.'

'*Wee* being the operative word. I hate the way the big designers get to dress the main windows now. It's so... *commercial.*'

'I know,' said Edie, hiding a smile at the art student's dismay and forcing her mind away from the past. She'd never got to college herself and had worked her way up the ranks to be a creative display artist. 'That's the way it is now, and I'm sure they'll be beautiful.'

'Yes, but they won't be *magical.*'

Privately Edie agreed. She too loved the magic and fantasy surrounding Christmas. She loved everything about Christmas. She was trying to create a little of that magic in this window, in spite of the fact that not many people would see it.

But, times had changed, and now the big fashion designers had more sway than the in-house creatives—especially at Christmas time.

She pulled out another box full of decorations and said, 'Right, we'll have a quick tea break and then get started with this lot. The window has to be finished by this evening.'

Jimmy mock saluted her. 'Aye aye, boss.'

Edie smiled at his cheeky grin as he escaped for his break. She looked at her watch and sighed. She knew she should take a break too, but if they wanted this window to be finished... She decided to keep going.

As soon as her mind was occupied with nothing more than unwrapping decorations, though, it invariably wandered back to the man—to *him*.

Edie looked up at the drapes suspiciously. She got up from the stool she'd perched on and went over cautiously, peeking out through a gap.

Of course the street was empty now. Strange to feel disappointed. And silly. Maybe she'd conjured him up out of some subconscious fantasy she'd never admitted to harbouring?

Edie pulled the curtains closed firmly and turned around, ready to put all random thoughts of disturbing men and memories out of her mind. She heard a sound and looked up with a smile on her face, expecting it to be Jimmy.

But it wasn't Jimmy. The smile promptly slid off her face.

Her supervisor, Helen, was standing in the doorway to the window space and behind her was...*him*. Even taller and more intimidating than she remembered. Not a fantasy. *Real.*

Helen, a no-nonsense blonde woman, came in, looking more than a little flushed and starry-eyed. And she was married with four children.

'Edie, I'd like to introduce you to someone.'

Edie's feet were glued to the floor. She could not believe this was happening.

And through the shock all she could think was, *Would he recognise her?* Her rational brain told her, *Of course not.* They'd barely spoken that night. She'd looked far different from how she looked now. And yet she couldn't deny the tripping of her pulse, the breathless sense of anticipation.

Her boss said, 'Edie, this is Mr Sebastio Rivas—Mr Rivas, this is Edie Munroe, one of our display artists.'

She stepped forward. The space, which was small anyway, now felt Lilliputian. Edie forced herself to look at him and her heart thudded to a stop. He was exactly how she remembered. Albeit slightly more groomed. His hair was still too long, but not as messy. The top button of his shirt was closed and his tie was pristine. She felt the strangest impulse to loosen it for him, as if she could sense that he felt constricted.

*Crazy.* He was a stranger. He had been then, and he still was. He was looking at her intently, but with no apparent spark of recognition. She wasn't sure if she was disappointed or relieved.

He held out his hand. It was big and masculine. She had a memory flash of that hand on her bare upper arm, steadying her. When she'd walked over to him in the club someone had bumped into her from behind, pitching her forward. His hand had circled her whole arm.

She realised that he was looking at her a little quizzically and that her boss was clearing her throat discreetly.

Mortified to have been caught in her moment, Edie quickly put her hand in his. It disappeared. That same jolt of electricity she'd felt four years ago sizzled in her blood and she pulled her hand back, doing her best to hide her reaction. And her shock.

'It's nice to meet you.'

She forced herself to look at him again. She noticed how grey his eyes were. Almost like steel. He had long dark lashes that only enhanced his physicality. Much like that ridiculously sensual mouth.

'It's a pleasure to meet you, Miss Munroe.'

Her toes curled at his deep and accented voice.

Her boss spoke. 'Mr Rivas has a proposition for you, Edie. Will you come with us to discuss it?'

She knew this wasn't a request. 'Of course. Jimmy will be back soon—he can get on with the rest of the decorating.'

Her boss made a small approving noise and went back out into the main shop. Sebastio Rivas indicated for Edie to go before him. She slipped out through the door, acutely conscious of him behind her, and she spotted more than one woman do a double-take as they walked past.

It brought back a flood of memories from that night. The way her heart had been pounding so hard after she'd walked over to him. Pounding with desire and nerves. It had been at that moment when someone had jostled her from behind and she'd pitched forward helplessly.

He'd put his hand around her arm to steady her and looked at her. 'Who *are* you?' His voice had been sharp. Almost accusatory.

Edie had stuttered out, 'N-no one. I just… I wanted to come and speak to you. I saw you…from across the room. You were looking at me too…and I thought… I thought you might want to speak to me…'

His gaze had swept her up and down with an almost clinical disregard. The connection that had borne her aloft to do such an audacious thing had suddenly felt very tenuous. Suddenly she'd been very aware of her hot itchy head and the skimpy dress that felt far *too* skimpy.

She'd also become acutely conscious of the thick VIP rope, separating him and his friends from everyone else. And her. She'd become aware of the stunning women orbiting around him—women Edie couldn't hope to compete with. Women with abundant curves and thick luxurious hair. Confident.

One of those women had come up to the man and slid an arm through his, pressing close. He'd glanced down at her, and then back to Edie, letting her arm go while saying, 'There's nothing for you here. You should run along.'

Edie had stood there, her arm tingling from his touch and her insides seizing with humiliation that she'd got it so wrong. He'd pulled the woman into his body and bent his head to kiss her, so explicitly that the men in his party had started cat-calling and wolf-whistling.

It had taken witnessing that final humiliation before Edie had turned blindly away and pushed her way back through the crowd...

'Sorry, I'll just be a moment.'

Edie blinked. She hadn't even noticed the journey to her boss's office, or the fact that Helen had obviously been called away by another staff member. But suddenly she became aware, as the door closed behind her, that she was now in a tiny room with Sebastio Rivas.

She'd only known who he was after she'd realised that he and all his friends were the Argentinian rugby team. After she'd got home that night she'd looked them up on the internet to find out that he was the captain. Their most prized asset. And the world's most successful rugby fly half.

Sebastio Rivas was looking at her.

Edie pushed aside the onslaught of memories and cleared her throat. 'Er… Helen said you had a…proposition?'

Instead of answering her question he asked, 'Your accent—where is it from?'

Edie's face grew warm. 'It's Scottish. I'm from a town just outside Edinburgh.'

He was looking at her so intently that she held her breath for a moment—he couldn't possibly be remembering her… could he?

But then he said, 'I do have a proposition, Miss Munroe. I want you to come and decorate my house for Christmas.'

It took a second for his words to sink in, they'd come so far out of left field. Edie's mouth opened and shut again, in shock. Opened again. 'I… I'm afraid I don't do private work… I work for the store. This is our busiest time.'

'Nevertheless, I'd like you to work for *me*.'

His tone suggested that he fully expected to be obeyed. Edie's hackles went up. As if she needed reminding that he was a man used to issuing orders…

*There's nothing for you here…run along.*

She crossed her arms over her chest and saw his eyes drop there momentarily, before rising to meet hers again. She hated feeling self-conscious, but it was hard when she knew she was…*lacking*. Small breasts, slim hips. And she'd been even skinnier four years ago.

Edie had put on weight and filled out since that time, but she'd never be able to compete with the kind of woman he evidently preferred, if the tall buxom woman he'd kissed that night had been an example of his tastes. No wonder he'd told Edie to *run along*.

That whole weird connection thing she'd felt? Clearly it had all been in her head…and it was even more mortifying to think of it now. She was thankful he didn't remember her.

'I'm afraid that's just not possible. I'm contracted to work here.'

'I'll match whatever your pay is for a year and triple it.'

Edie's breath stalled for a moment at the audacious offer—and the prospect of making more money than she'd ever made in her life. But then she shook her head.

'I'm sorry, Mr Rivas. I can't just leave and work for you… I'd lose my job if I left them in the lurch at Christmas.' She saw an obdurate expression come over his face and blurted out, '*Why* do you want me to decorate your house? There are companies that hire out staff to do that specific job every year.'

She could see the flare of irritation in his pewter eyes—more evidence that he wasn't used to being questioned. She had the curious urge to stand up to him at all costs, not even sure why it was so important. Maybe because she didn't want to be so dismissable this time?

'I have a large house in Richmond, where I'm due to host some social functions in the run-up to Christmas. I saw your work. I like the level of detail you've put into a window that—let's face it—not many people will even see.'

Edie flushed, not expecting the compliment, nor that he would have recognised that their efforts were largely in vain. 'I'm trained to dress windows and spaces around the store. I've never dressed an entire house before.'

Edie knew a couple of her colleagues did work on the side for some clients—decorating their Christmas trees and the like. But not a whole actual house. And he'd mentioned that it was in Richmond, where houses were mansions.

He shrugged that aside. 'I just need to dress the rooms being used for the functions and the exterior. I have no desire to decorate the entire property.'

His mouth tightened, as if in distaste at the very thought,

and Edie had to push down her curiosity to know why. 'But it's just three weeks to Christmas—'

'And I have my first function the week after next. So you can see why speed is of the essence.'

Edie felt bewildered. 'Why me?'

He countered, 'Why not?'

# CHAPTER TWO

SEBASTIO COULD SEE the woman worrying her lower lip between her teeth, and he had to curb an urge to reach out and free that lip. He quashed the desire. If she was going to work for him then theirs would be a purely professional relationship. He felt a pang of regret and quashed that too.

She wasn't his type. She might have sparked something, but surely it was just the resurgence of his dormant libido. Slightly above average height, she was even more delicate up close. Yet once again he had an impression of steeliness underneath her slender frame.

Their dialogue bore that out. He wasn't used to meeting anyone who didn't say *How high?* when he asked them to jump. In fact, she had an air of palpable reluctance to deal with him. It intrigued him as much as it irritated him—not a reception he was used to.

Sebastio forced himself to focus. He needed this woman to take care of things he didn't want to think about. The more reluctant she was, the more determined he became.

He spoke with a patient tone that belied his frustration that this conversation wasn't going as easily as he'd planned. 'Are you telling me you couldn't do with a considerable bonus in the run-up to Christmas?'

He glanced up and down at her very functional but boring workwear. He could appreciate that she had the kind of elegant figure that would look good in anything. And suddenly he had a desire to see her in something altogether more feminine and soft.

She glared at him now, and Sebastio's desire sky-rocketed. It mocked his assertion that she wasn't his type. Apparently, right now, she was.

'It's not about whether or not I need a bonus. I'm afraid it's just not an option to walk away from my job here and work for you, no matter how much you're offering.'

Edie had a vision at that precise moment of her parents up in Scotland. They both looked a lot older than their years and her conscience pricked. That was because of her. They'd worried about her so much... And then, just when her father had retired and should have been looking forward to some time off, he'd had a heart attack. The Caribbean cruise they'd spent their savings on had had to be cancelled, and with no insurance and an indifferent travel company they'd lost out on the trip of a lifetime.

With the kind of money Mr Rivas was offering so casually Edie could afford to send them on three cruises! And she could afford to pay for private health insurance— something that would make them a lot less anxious in the future.

But there was no way she would jeopardise her job to work for a man who was arrogant enough to demand that she do so. She ignored another prick of her conscience telling her it was for far more varied and personal reasons that she felt disinclined to work for him.

'I'm sorry, Mr Rivas. As intriguing as your offer is, I'm afraid I can't just leave my job here at the store.'

'Well, yes, you can, actually—for a brief time.'

Edie blinked and turned around. She hadn't even heard her boss come back into the room, she'd been so engrossed by the man in front of her.

Her stomach fell. 'But, Helen—'

The women lifted her hand. 'Mr Rivas is newly located to London from Argentina, and we welcome him as an esteemed client. We would be more than happy to release you to work privately for him in the run-up to Christmas, with the understanding that once the work is complete you will return to your job here.'

Edie couldn't believe what she was hearing. Do a private commission for Sebastio Rivas *and* keep her job? He had to be verging on royalty to precipitate this kind of fawning... She'd never seen any sports star get this level of treatment before.

Edie tried again. 'Helen, I really don't think that—'

But the woman was now ignoring Edie and opening the door to let Sebastio Rivas out of the office, saying officiously, 'Leave it with us, Mr Rivas. We'll do everything necessary to get Edie released from her schedule here as soon as possible.'

The door closed on an image of Sebastio Rivas looking directly at Edie with unmistakable challenge. She shivered at what that challenge might be—to do a job, or to let her know he'd noticed her reacting to his presence and could see all the way through her skin to where there was a pulse of something intimate.

It reminded her of that night in the club, when she'd felt as if he was looking right into her soul. It was galling that he had the same effect on her now.

Her boss turned around to face Edie. 'Do you have any idea who that is?'

Edie swallowed, feeling curiously flat now that he had left the room. 'He's a rugby player with the Argentinian rugby team.'

Helen waved a dismissive hand. 'He retired as a rugby player a few years ago. Sebastio Rivas is now CEO of

Rivas Bank—he's descended from one of the most powerful banking families in the world.'

Edie absorbed this. That would explain his air of arrogance and entitlement. He came from a rarefied world.

Her boss went on to explain breathlessly what an important addition to London society he was. How generous he was to charity. Then she said, 'So, the fact that he wants *you* to decorate his house for Christmas is obviously something we will facilitate.'

Edie recognised Helen's steely tone. She also recognised that this was an amazing opportunity. She'd been offered a ridiculous amount of money and her supervisor had just assured her that her job would still be there when she came back.

So why was she so reluctant?

*Because*, said a small voice, *that man rejected you at a time when you ached to be normal and know what it was to feel like to be a woman. And because he's a reminder that you still don't know what it is to be a real woman.*

It was humiliating to think that within the last four years she'd obviously changed and matured on many levels, but on a very private and intimate level she was the same girl she had been that night. Gauche and inexperienced. Desperate to fit in. Desperate for experience. Desperate to *live*.

'Edie? If you're reluctant to do this I can always find someone else…'

Edie's attention snapped back to the present and her boss, who was looking at her, clearly impatient to have this dealt with. Edie knew she'd have no hesitation in asking the next person.

A determination settled in her gut not to allow this opportunity to slip away just because seeing Sebastio Rivas again had been disconcerting. To say the least.

'No, of course I'll do it. I'd be crazy not to.'

Helen smiled approvingly. 'Good. If you like, you can go home early—you'll be very busy up till Christmas. Mr Rivas said he'd send further instructions via his assistant.'

Edie didn't fancy the long bus journey home to her bedsit in north London, with too much time to think about things, so she said, 'No, I'll finish the window with Jimmy. It's almost done anyway.'

Helen shrugged. 'Whatever you want, Edie. Most people would jump at the chance to go home early.'

Edie smiled weakly. She wasn't most people and she didn't need the reminder.

For the rest of the day she and Jimmy worked in companionable harmony. Thankfully he didn't seem to notice her tension. When they were leaving work he asked if she'd like to join him and his friends at a nearby bar, but she smiled and declined. Her brain was addled after everything that had happened that day. Seeing Rivas again. Feeling the same things.

As she sat on the crowded bus, heading north from the centre of town, she told herself to stop being so trepiditious. Maybe getting to know Sebastio Rivas a little would help her to topple him from the almost mythic place he'd taken up in her consciousness, where no other man could touch him.

After all, he hadn't ever known her circumstances, had he? That night in the club she'd been just another woman approaching him for a sliver of attention… He couldn't possibly have known just how fragile she'd been then.

But she wasn't fragile any more.

Edie forced her mind away from the past and pulled her phone out of her pocket when she felt it vibrate. There was a text message from Helen, with an address in Richmond. Sebastio Rivas's address.

Her heart thumped when she read it.

You're to meet Sebastio Rivas at his house tomorrow at ten a.m. He'll talk you through what needs to be done and his legal team will draw up a temporary work contract. Good luck and Happy Christmas, Edie! Helen

Once again Edie was stunned that her boss had sanctioned this move. Albeit temporarily. But, in fairness, it wasn't as if Marrotts was short of display artists. She was one of many. And of course it would enhance their reputation to loan out one of their staff to a new and illustrious client.

Edie quickly did an internet search on the address in Richmond, and five minutes later wished she hadn't. It was an old hunting lodge that looked more like a mansion than a lodge, set in acres and acres of its own grounds. There were even wild deer. Her experience was in dressing spaces that ranged between ten and twenty-five square feet. Not grand country mansions!

She felt a flare of panic and doused it, telling herself that she'd overcome far bigger challenges in the past. She wasn't going to allow Sebastio Rivas to see that she was daunted by this project. He'd told her to *run along* once before. She wouldn't give him the opportunity to do it again.

The following morning, Edie turned a corner in the long winding drive that led up to the house in Richmond, cursing herself for assuring the security guard at the gate that she wouldn't mind the walk. He'd tried to get her to wait for a groundsman to give her a lift but she'd insisted, needing to get her wits about her. She hadn't realised it would take quite so long, though.

And now she stopped in her tracks. Dazzled by the sight before her. No picture could have done justice to the low winter sun glinting off hundreds of windows and the sheer stately magnificence of the house.

It had two levels, and an elegantly grand front entrance. She could make out what looked like manicured gardens at the back, and as far as the eye could see to the front were rolling grounds, with a wood in the distance.

As she approached the front entrance, feeling more and more intimidated, the huge front door opened and a dapper older gentleman dressed in a smart suit appeared.

He came down the steps, smiling and holding out his hand. 'You must be Edie.'

She came forward, 'Yes.' She shook his hand. He had an accent that she guessed was from Italy.

'I'm Matteo, Mr Rivas's housekeeper. He's on his way from his office in London, but some of his assistants are here to go through the contract with you in the meantime.'

Edie barely had time to catch her breath before her coat and bag were taken and she was being ushered into a bright office off the entrance hall, where two men and a woman stood up to greet her. They were sleek and officious. Polite but brisk. No doubt they had better things to be doing back in the city.

She'd just signed on the dotted line, and was still reeling with the knowledge that she was going to be paid a fortune for what was effectively a little over three weeks' work, when a distinctive *thwack-thwack* sound came from outside.

She looked out of the window to see a sleek black helicopter landing at the back of the property. She shivered slightly.

Sebastio Rivas's assistants packed up their things and said goodbye to Edie, and then they swept out, leaving her standing in the room, waiting for the man himself.

As she waited, the tension inside her grew.

What was she doing here? Thinking she could step into

Sebastio Rivas's world like this? This was on another level. The kind of level people like Edie never got close to. The man had taken a helicopter to get here, for crying out loud! She'd spent the best part of two hours on a packed Tube and had then taken a taxi from the station.

At that moment she heard a noise and looked to the door, to see Sebastio Rivas easily filling its frame with his tall, broad body. His black hair was unruly, which she guessed was from the helicopter. He wore a three-piece suit and in spite of the messy hair he looked every inch a successful titan of international finance.

And yet she could sense something far more elemental underneath—the barely leashed power of the fierce athlete he'd once been. It was very provocative.

He came into the room. 'You've signed the contract?'

She nodded, wishing she was wearing something more daring than plain black trousers and a white shirt under a sleeveless grey top. She'd never felt less feminine.

*Yes, you have*, reminded a voice. When the same man had looked at her as if she was an irritation that night in the club.

Sebastio glanced at his watch. 'I need to be back in the city for a meeting before lunch, so let me show you around now.'

Edie followed him out through the door, hating that he made her feel so self-conscious. She tried her best to look around and not be distracted by his athletic build.

He was pointing out the entrance hall. 'This will be the first point of entry for guests, so I'd like something suitably festive in here. A big tree. Lights.'

Edie took out a notebook from her back pocket, and a pen, and started making notes.

Sebastio turned around and saw Edie's downbent head as she wrote in a small notebook. Her hair shone bright auburn in the sunlight streaming through the window. She couldn't have been less enticing in her very plain clothes, but from the moment he'd walked in and seen her, awareness had sizzled in his blood.

She was having the same effect she'd had on him the previous day. So it wasn't an anomaly. Or an aberration. It was irritating as hell—especially when Sebastio had always been in control of his libido.

He also felt something tugging on his memory...that vague sense of déjà-vu he'd had yesterday. *Had* he met her somewhere before? It was relatively likely—especially in his rugby-playing days, when his social scene had been far more hectic and debauched.

He was almost about to ask her, but then he told himself that it was four years of celibacy playing tricks on his mind, telling him he was attracted to this sprite. Telling him he might *know* her.

Four years of celibacy. *Was that enough of a penance?* Sebastio felt bleak.

Edie looked up at that moment, and her blue eyes widened as if she could see his thoughts. Sebastio cursed his reaction. He did not want to desire her.

The women he was famous for favouring poured their curvaceous bodies into designer dresses and had long luxurious hair. Not a slender frame that looked as if it might snap in a strong breeze and a bright auburn cap of feathery hair that should have made Edie look androgynous but only enhanced her delicate femininity.

All he wanted from her was to save him a lot of hassle by creating the illusion that he didn't despise Christmas.

*Liar*, whispered a voice. He ignored it.

He reminded himself that she was his employee now, and out of bounds. 'Let's keep going,' he said curtly.

Edie followed Sebastio, stinging a little at the tone of

his voice. It was as if she'd done something to irritate him. She was almost inclined to remind him that he'd brought her here, but he'd stopped in the middle of the main reception room now and turned to face her again.

She quickly schooled her features into something she hoped was bland. She hated Sebastio Rivas at that moment, for making her feel so many things at once. Prickly, *aware*, defensive.

She looked away from him and said briskly, 'You said you have a meeting to get to— Why don't you show me what you want done?'

For a long moment there was silence, and then Sebastio responded, 'You really don't want to be here, do you?'

Edie looked at him in shock. Had she been so transparent?

He folded his arms. 'But what I can't figure out is why it feels like you've taken a personal dislike to me, when we don't even know each other.'

Edie balked. She could feel the heat rising over her chest and up her neck into her cheeks. She wanted to squirm. Her inability to hide her reaction was irritating in the extreme.

Stiffly she said, 'I don't know you enough to like or dislike you.'

Which, technically, was true. After all, they'd only really met before for a few moments. Not that she'd ever admit it, in case he remembered the skinny girl in the badly fitting wig and too-short dress who'd tried to chat him up so ineffectually.

'Would you really prefer if I hadn't asked you to take on this assignment?'

She forced herself to look at him, even though it was hard when those grey eyes were narrowed on her and looking at her so intently. She took an inward breath. She needed to let go of whatever impression she'd had of him from before. It wasn't his fault she was still carrying it around like a weight.

'I won't deny that the space is daunting. But, no, I'm glad you asked me. It's good to get out of my comfort zone.'

He arched a brow. 'Personally I've always seen comfort zones as the death of progress or achievement.'

Edie could well imagine that. She doubted a man like Sebastio Rivas had ever been in a comfort zone in his life. She shivered a little at the prospect of going so far outside her own.

He unfolded his arms. 'I will just have to do my best to garner your favour, Edie.'

The thought of him trying to charm her made panic spike. 'Not every woman on the planet has to like you.'

The words had spilled out before Edie could censor them, and she looked at Sebastio aghast, expecting him to storm out and fire her on the spot. Instead his head fell back and he let out a full-throated laugh.

When he looked back at her his eyes were gleaming with genuine amusement and her chest grew tight. He looked years younger and less intense when he smiled.

'Indeed, they don't.' He glanced at his watch. 'As you pointed out, I'm under pressure for time—so why don't we get on with it?'

Edie's conscience smarted. He hadn't really deserved her waspish reply, but he put her on edge and made her feel jittery. She hadn't been expecting that response. It disarmed her. And then she felt guilty. Had she subconsciously wanted to provoke him into firing her because that would be easier than dealing with him again and facing up to how he made her feel?

Edie looked around the room they'd entered and their previous exchange was forgotten in the face of what could be described only as majesty.

It was a massive room, with an enormous stone fireplace at one end. An ornate coat of arms hung above it. Huge chandeliers. A wall of windows with the longest curtains she'd ever seen in her life, made of heavy luxurious velvet. The parquet floor was covered in oriental rugs.

Edie wondered how on earth he had thought she could do this. After all, he'd only seen a tiny display—a few branches, leaves and artfully cut-out decorations!

Sebastio stood in the middle of the room, perfectly in proportion with the space around him. But for once his sheer masculine beauty couldn't distract her as the full enormity of what he was asking of her sank in.

'Look, I'm truly flattered that you liked my display enough to think I could do this…but I don't want to mislead you. This is way beyond my capabilities in such a short space of time.' She started to back out through the door. 'You need to hire professionals who are used to dealing with a project of this size. Why have you left it so late?'

The question landed like a lead weight in Sebastio's gut. Because he didn't want to be doing this at all. But he could read the panic in Edie's eyes, and he suspected that unless he was honest she'd bolt.

'Because;' he said heavily, 'I detest Christmas.'

The panic faded to be replaced by something else. Curiosity? Sympathy? Cursing himself for giving in to an impulse to be *honest*, because it would only lead to questions he wasn't prepared to answer, Sebastio went into damage limitation mode.

'What about this? I'll hire professionals who have expertise and resources in this area, but I want you to design the decorations and oversee everything. So in essence you'll be the creative designer and you'll have all the help you need.'

She still looked as if she was ready to turn and run, and

Sebastio didn't like the sense of desperation he felt to convince her at all costs.

He said, 'I know you've probably never project-managed anything this big before, but really it's just a matter of being clear about what you want and delegating. Would it help if you could have the young man who was working on the window with you?'

Her mouth closed and he could see her brain whirring as she took that in. She relaxed perceptibly.

'Well...that would be helpful...to have someone I know here.'

Sebastio thought of something then, and asked sharply, 'Are you in a relationship with him?'

He couldn't recall the features of the skinny young man, but he was already regretting saying that he could be part of this commission.

Edie looked affronted. 'No! Jimmy is gay. Not that it's any business of yours.'

Some of the tension in Sebastio's chest immediately eased. 'I think you can do this job, Edie. I wouldn't ask you if I thought you weren't capable. I'm not in the habit of hiring or working with incompetents.'

That made him think of the cohesive unit of the rugby team around him, all working as one to the best of their ability. He pushed down the pang of regret. The ever-present guilt.

Edie was biting her lip again, and Sebastio had to fight the urge to close the distance between them and crush that lush mouth under his, seeking to dilute his memories as much as anything else.

*Because he wanted her.*

He cursed himself. He hadn't needed to exercise restraint for a long time—if ever—but he had to exercise it now. He couldn't jeopardise his successful acceptance into

European society just because his hormones had decided to come back to life.

He backed away, putting distance between them. 'I'll show you the rest of the rooms to be decorated…'

Edie dutifully followed Sebastio as he took her through yet more rooms with the same football field dimensions. She couldn't help wondering why he detested Christmas so much. But then she told herself it was none of her business. Not everyone liked the festive season. She knew that. It could be hard for people who didn't have family around them, and if Sebastio Rivas was spending Christmas in London then maybe he had family issues…

The shock and trepidation were wearing off slightly as she focused on what Sebastio was saying about each room, what he wanted, and in spite of her earlier sense of panic she actually began to imagine the rooms dressed for Christmas, filled with guests. She was surprised at how easily images were coming to her—considering the proportions!

'So you'll do it, then?' Sebastio asked.

They were in a ballroom that had French doors leading out to a terrace overlooking a vast manicured garden, complete with fountain.

Would she do it? Could she?

She realised now that she did want to do this. It would be a huge challenge—beyond anything she'd ever done before.

*It's not just for the challenge, though, is it?* asked a wicked little voice.

It was because of the way this man made her feel—alive and aware. Exactly the way he'd made her feel that night four years ago. As if just looking at him and connecting with him, even so fleetingly and painfully, had given her some vital injection of life-force. Something she'd been afraid she'd never feel again.

She knew it wasn't appropriate to be feeling like this

about a man who was hiring her to do a job, but it would be her own illicit secret. After all, it wasn't as if Sebastio would ever find out—she wasn't remotely in his league. She hadn't been then and she wasn't now. That hadn't changed.

She looked at him and tipped up her chin. 'If you're willing to take a risk on hiring me to do this job then I promise I'll do it to the best of my ability.'

He inclined his head, the corner of his mouth tipping up ever so slightly. 'I can't ask for more than that.'

He looked at his watch and became brisk.

'I'll ask my team to liaise with you regarding hiring a suitable firm to help you, and I'll negotiate with your supervisor at Marrotts to let Jimmy join you.'

Once again Edie marvelled at what it must be like to be powerful enough to make people do your bidding, no matter how big the ask. In the space of less than twenty-four hours he'd comprehensively turned her life upside down, and it was disconcerting but also...thrilling.

As if he had issued a psychic command, Matteo appeared with Sebastio's coat and a briefcase, handing them over. He said, 'The pilot is ready when you are.'

Matteo disappeared again, and Sebastio looked at her after he'd pulled on his coat. 'I can offer you a lift back into the city, if you'd like?'

Edie blanched and then squeaked out, 'In the helicopter?'

He nodded. 'Ever been in one before?'

She shook her head, and then gabbled, 'No, it's fine, Mr Rivas. I should stay and make some notes. I can take the train back.'

*Coward!* whispered a little voice. She ignored it. Taking a helicopter ride with Sebastio Rivas would only compound the conflicting things he made her feel. She needed to keep her feet on the ground. Where she belonged.

He made a face. 'Please, call me Sebastio. "Mr Rivas" makes me sound like my father, and he's dead.'

Edie felt an immediate burst of compassion. 'Oh… I'm sorry. Was it recent?'

But Sebastio's face was impassive. 'A year ago. We weren't close.' He was turning to go and said, 'Are you sure about the ride?'

Edie nodded. She was far too intrigued by this man as it was. And this nugget of information made him even more intriguing.

'Very well, I'll have my driver come and pick you up and take you back into town—just let Matteo know when you'd like to leave.'

'Thank you, Mr—' She stopped and could feel herself grow warm.

Sebastio stopped too, a glint coming into his eye. 'Go on, Edie…say it. You won't turn to stone.'

She crushed the sense of exposure and took a breath, willing her voice to sound totally cool. 'Sebastio. Thank you, Sebastio.'

He started walking backwards, his mouth tipping up on one side in a wicked smile. 'See? That wasn't so hard, was it?'

Edie watched him depart and scowled at his broad back. He was making fun of her. Her fascination with him must be blindingly obvious.

She whirled around and stalked back into the room they'd just left, and when she heard the sound of the helicopter taking off she refused to look out of the window because she had the very irrational sense that even from here she'd see a mocking smile on his face.

'Just a bit higher, Jimmy. That's it.'

Edie looked up at the massive Christmas tree that stood,

almost twenty feet tall, at the foot of the grand marble staircase in the main reception hall. It was finally dressed.

Jimmy climbed down the ladder and stood with her. In a moment of doubt, she said, 'You don't think it's too rustic, do you?'

He shook his head. 'No, it's perfect. Really different and unique. You've done an amazing job, Edie. The place looks stunning.'

She felt a spurt of pride. But she just wasn't sure if it was exactly what Sebastio Rivas had been looking for. She hadn't seen him again for the whole week, and since she'd agreed on a firm to help her with the decorating she hadn't had time to think.

Jimmy coughed discreetly beside her and she looked at him, to see him jerking his head slightly. She felt the small hairs on the back of her neck stand up just as she turned around to see Sebastio behind her, looking up at the tree.

He had obviously recently arrived, and was dressed in another three-piece suit and an overcoat. An immediate flash of heat right through to her core made a mockery of the fact that she'd tried to convince herself all week that her reaction to him had been a fleeting thing, based on a potent memory.

It didn't feel fleeting now.

It felt as if her body had been in a dormant state all week until this moment.

He looked at her and Jimmy. 'Why are you working on a Saturday?'

Edie felt ridiculously defensive. 'It's just the two of us. There's so much to do and it's easier to finish things off when there's no one else around. Jimmy is heading home now.'

Jimmy looked at Edie, as if to say, *I can stay if you want?* but she shook her head and he backed away.

'See you on Monday morning.'

'Thanks, Jimmy.'

When she and Sebastio were alone he said, 'You're not heading home?'

'Well, I wasn't going to—not right now. There are still some things I'm tweaking. Your first dinner party is next Tuesday,' she reminded him a little primly.

His mouth quirked slightly. 'I'm well aware of that.'

She flushed. She noticed that he hadn't said anything positive about the decorations, but also he wasn't saying anything negative. And then something struck her. It was Saturday and he was obviously here for the weekend. Possibly with someone in tow. A lover?

As that suspicion sank in a wave of embarrassment washed over her. Edie immediately started to back away. 'I'm so sorry. I just assumed we could have the run of the place until the first party, but of course you're home for the weekend—no doubt looking for privacy. I'll get my things…leave you in peace.'

She turned to leave, but her arm was caught in a big hand and she stopped, her face flaming now. She turned back to face him and he was staring down at her.

'What on earth are you talking about?'

Edie wanted to crawl into a hole. This was far too reminiscent of another time and place. *Run along...* And she really didn't want to hang around to see him kiss whatever stunningly beautiful woman he'd brought home for the weekend for recreational purposes. Which was none of her business.

'Obviously you want your privacy for the weekend.'

He frowned again, shaking his head. 'What…?'

Now she was feeling angry, on top of embarrassed. She pulled her arm free. 'Just let me go home and I'll leave you and your…guest alone.'

She'd started walking away again when she heard him behind her.

'Edie—*stop*.'

Reluctantly she did. He came and stood in front of her, and against every effort her insides clenched in response to his sheer presence. His evocative scent. This was so humiliating. Any second now she expected to hear a woman's voice, calling for her lover.

He was frowning. 'Are you suggesting I have someone here with me?'

He sounded so incredulous that Edie just looked at him for a moment. 'Don't you?'

He shook his head, and a curious expression crossed his face—half angry, half frustrated—before he said, 'No, I'm alone.'

Now Edie wanted the ground to swallow her for an entirely different reason. She'd just exposed herself spectacularly.

She swallowed. 'Sorry… I just assumed…'

He sounded grim. 'Well, you assumed wrong. The reason I was asking why you were still here is because you shouldn't be working at the weekend.'

Sebastio looked down at Edie and saw the evidence of her embarrassment on her flushed face. It made him feel alternately irritated and aroused. Why did he always feel as if he'd insulted her in some way?

He'd got caught up in a round of social engagements in the past week, and hadn't been able to make it back to the house. Which in any other circumstances wouldn't have bothered him in the slightest. But knowing *she* was there… that was a different matter.

He'd been in Paris the previous evening, at an exclusive charity ball, surrounded by the crème de la crème of European society. The most beautiful people in the world.

Certainly the most beautiful women. All vying for his attention. And not one had sparked his libido like she had... and did.

As soon as he'd walked in here this morning and seen her he'd felt the resurgence of desire. Igniting his nerve-endings. Making him hard.

But then he'd noticed something else. Shadows under her eyes.

His voice was rough. 'You look tired.'

Her eyes flashed, and perversely that eased Sebastio's conscience.

'It's been a busy week. We've all been putting in long hours to get the work done in time, and with the commute...'

'Commute?'

She nodded. 'Well, yes...'

'Where do you live?'

She blinked, as if his question had taken her aback. 'North London—Islington.'

Sebastio cursed under his breath. She might as well be in Paris. Even if he had his driver ferry her back and forth every day it would still be a huge commute. No wonder she looked tired.

He made a split-second decision. 'You're going to move in here for the duration of your contract.'

# CHAPTER THREE

SHOCK REVERBERATED THROUGH EDIE. *'You're going to move in here...'* It wasn't a question.

Sebastio was looking at her as if he was enjoying watching her reaction. And then he said musingly, 'You've got a very expressive face. It's amazingly refreshing.'

Edie scowled and folded her arms. She didn't like to be reminded of how gauche she must seem to a man like him, who was undoubtedly surrounded by sophisticates who knew better than to let every thought be read like a cloud passing across the sky.

'Are you always this bossy?'

He bit back a smile. 'I think it's my duty to ensure your health and safety.'

She looked at Sebastio suspiciously. She knew her commute was a bit ridiculous—even Jimmy had asked her how she was doing it. He lived in South London, so Richmond was handy for him. He'd offered her his couch to sleep on, but she preferred to sleep well for a few hours rather than badly for longer!

Sebastio was waiting for her reply. He really meant it.

She unfolded her arms. 'I can't just move in here... It's not...appropriate.'

'Says who?'

'Me!' Edie fired back.

'I'll hardly be here, if that's what you're worried about.'

She managed to stop herself from pointing out that he was here now.

'I just don't think it's right.' And then, before she could stop her runaway mouth, she was asking, 'Why buy a property like this if you're hardly ever here?'

Sebastio tensed. No one ever questioned him. And her question cut far too close to the bone. There were myriad reasons why he'd bought this place—chief of which were to do with its privacy and space, which appealed to his need to hide from the world and his ever-present guilt. However, he'd also bought it for its potential for entertaining. And its exclusivity.

*But those aren't the only reasons*, whispered a mocking voice.

No. They weren't. And he hated to admit it—even to himself. Hated to admit that in spite of the fact that he'd never felt as if he'd had a home, he wanted to create one. Some place where he might feel some measure of peace or atonement. When he didn't deserve atonement. At all.

Not when he'd mocked Victor and Maya for their happy domestic idyll just moments before he'd been intrumental in wrecking that idyll for ever.

'That's none of your business,' he said now, with more bite than he'd intended.

Edie was immediately contrite. She'd overstepped the boundaries, unsettled by this man. 'I'm sorry. Of course it's none of my business.'

'Look, it's far more practical for you to stay here for the next couple of weeks. There's really no need for you to do that commute every day.'

Edie knew he was talking sense. He sounded eminently reasonable. If she insisted on protesting she'd look silly. And he might wonder why she was so reluctant.

'Okay,' she conceded finally. 'You're right—it does make sense.'

Sebastio said, 'Good. I'll have my driver take you home now and he'll bring you back with your things.'

Edie's heart thumped. 'Today? But there's no need—'

Sebastio cut her off smoothly. 'Why not move in today? At least then you'll have the weekend to fully recuperate. There's a gym here, and a swimming pool. You might as well avail yourself of those amenities while you can.'

She closed her mouth. She'd heard some of the other staff mention the gym and the pool in awestruck voices, but she'd had no time to explore.

She saw the obdurate look on Sebastio's face. There was no point arguing. 'Fine.'

Now a look of amusement came over his starkly handsome features, elevating him from gorgeous to devastating.

'No need to sound so gratified.'

Edie flushed. Again. This man seemed to bring out the worst in her.

'Of course I'm grateful. It's incredibly generous of you.'

A few hours later Edie was standing in the middle of her new bedroom, absorbing the fact that she was really doing this. Sharing Sebastio's house. She grimaced. Except it wasn't really a *house* when there was enough room for a dozen football teams and their fans.

The bedroom was sumptuous and understated, decorated in tones of light blue and grey. A massive bed dominated the room, which had a luxurious ensuite bathroom and also a dressing room.

Edie had unpacked and hung up her few clothes, but the expanse of the dressing room only made them look more boring and pathetic. It was a room for shimmering gowns and hundreds of jewel-coloured shoes.

She didn't need the uncomfortable reminder that her encounter with Sebastio four years previously had affected her on many more levels than she liked to admit. Namely, her sense of femininity and her attractiveness to men. Maybe that was what always drew her up short on dates? She clammed up as much because of her own self-consciousness as anything they were doing or weren't doing.

*Or maybe*, said a mischievous voice, *they just hadn't been Sebastio.*

Edie rejected that utterly. It was too terrifying to contemplate. She couldn't have been in thrall to a man she'd met for mere minutes all this time. But even as she rejected it the knowledge settled in her gut like a lead weight.

The night she'd met Sebastio she'd felt like a fish out of water in that club, in spite of her happiness at the clear bill of health she'd been given. She'd been full of so many mixed emotions, and the throbbing music and heat of the club had compounded that turmoil inside her. Her friends had meant well, wanting to make it up to her because she'd missed out on her prom night... But really Edie hadn't been ready for a scene like that yet.

That was one of the reasons she'd connected so instantly with Sebastio. He too had looked as if he was set apart from his peers. A little lost. Except it had been a mirage. She'd projected her own feelings onto him.

And she needed to remember that now. She was here to work, not dream of owning silky dresses that would hang in her dressing room. Just because Sebastio had insisted she stay, it did not mean she was now a part of his world. Far from it.

Sebastio was standing at his study window on Monday morning, observing Edie as she helped her team bring in more boxes of decorations. She was smiling and laughing at something someone had said and it made something dark unfurl inside him—a desire for her to smile and laugh like that for *him*.

Somehow she'd managed to evade him over the weekend.

He'd asked her to join him for dinner, only to be informed that she'd already eaten.

He'd passed her on his way to the gym. She'd been pink-cheeked, with her short damp hair curling around her face, and he'd felt a burn low in his gut as he'd wondered if that was how she would look in the aftermath of passion. Sated and replete.

And he'd seen her striding purposefully out through the front door and into the grounds, as if on a mission to find lost treasure.

One thing was clear: her reluctance to be in his company.

As Edie disappeared from sight, and Sebastio turned away from the view, he clamped down on the hunger building inside him. Edie Munroe was not for him. She was altogether far too wholesome—and since when had he ever been attracted to *wholesome*? The one thing he couldn't be accused of was seducing innocents—and Edie was an innocent.

How much of an innocent he wasn't sure, but he didn't intend on finding out.

It was the evening of the first formal dinner party and Edie was in her room, watching the guests start to arrive. Most of the house-dressing staff had been released now. She would stay on-site to make sure that everything remained intact, and Jimmy would help her with redressing after each party. The others wouldn't return now until after Christmas, when the decorations would be taken down.

Sebastio had come and made an inspection of the

dressed main hall and other rooms earlier, and he'd shown neither pleasure nor distaste at the whimsical displays Edie had come up with. She'd been nervous about his reaction, because she'd used branches, leaves and vines from the surrounding woods for the centre of the dining table, interspersed with candles and red berries. It was rustic more than traditional.

She'd kept most of the other decorations on the subtle side, and infused the air with scents of delicate spices.

The massive Christmas tree in the main hall was probably the most traditional and opulent item, and when she'd turned on the lights everyone had gasped in wonder. But Sebastio had merely skimmed an eye over it.

He had at least acknowledged her team, if not her personally, by saying, 'You've all done a fantastic job—thank you.'

They'd left with big smiles and starry eyes. But Edie had felt deflated. They'd done Trojan work to get the house dressed in time! And yet what had she expected? Sebastio had never made any secret of the fact that he was merely doing this as a gesture, to conform with the festive season and dress his house accordingly. He'd admitted he hated Christmas. And she was just an employee.

But still... She'd felt as if they had some sort of connection.

And that was a very dangerous way to think, because him persuading her to do a job and making it easier for her by asking her to move in had nothing to do with anything other than facilitating that job.

For the whole weekend—even though she'd done her best to stay out of his way—she'd felt a little hum of electricity coursing through her blood. She had been all too aware that he was in the vicinity.

Matteo had come with an invitation for Edie to join Sebastio for dinner, but she'd assumed he was doing it merely to be polite, so she'd said no. Quite frankly, the thought of sharing any kind of intimate space with the man was alternately terrifying and thrilling.

A movement caught Edie's eye from down below and she saw a couple emerge from a sleek limousine. The man's hair was dark blond in the light and he was breathtakingly handsome. The woman was stunning. Tall and elegant, wearing a long fur coat under which Edie could see flashes of black silk. Her glossy dark hair was piled high in a chignon and diamonds sparkled at her ears. She was smiling up at him, and he was looking down at her with such indulgence that Edie's chest hurt.

From here she could hear the faint strains of classical music. She'd watched the quartet setting up earlier in the main hall, where she knew the guests were being served with champagne. She could also hear the hum of voices and deep laughter.

Edie didn't realise she had a hand on her chest to assuage the tightness until long after the glamorous couple had disappeared into the house. It was mortifying to admit it, but she felt envious. Deeply envious. She'd longed all throughout her illness to experience an evening like this—looking beautiful, *feeling* beautiful, on the arm of a handsome, attentive man.

Determined to put all such notions out of her head, Edie took the back route down to the kitchen, which was full of feverish activity as the staff catered for the dinner party upstairs. She pushed all pangs of envy aside, telling herself she was being ridiculous, and made herself a sandwich.

When Edie woke, hours later, there was no more noise. The party must have finished. She knew she wouldn't fall back to sleep easily. Her head had latched on to the bizarre fact that she'd forgotten to send some emails to her suppliers earlier.

Groaning, she got up and pulled a robe over her pyjamas. She could nip down to the office and send the emails and be back in bed within ten minutes.

As she made her way down in the half-light she imagined Sebastio's derisory look if he saw her in her pyjamas. No doubt the women he took to bed wore nothing but perfume. Maybe there was a woman in his bed now?

Edie groaned at herself. *Stop thinking about him!*

She went into the office and flicked a switch, blinking a little as she got used to the brighter light.

She went over to the computer and sat down, hitting a key so that it woke up. She'd sent the emails within a couple of minutes but then, just as she was about to close it down again, she found her fingers hovering uncertainly over the keyboard.

*Why* did Sebastio hate Christmas so much?

That and other questions tumbled around in Edie's head and she couldn't resist the temptation. Not when access to information was so tantalisingly close.

She quickly typed Sebastio's name into the search field before she lost her nerve.

The first thing that popped up was a screaming headline.

*Tragic head-on collision claims life of Maya Sanchez and leaves Victor Sanchez paralysed!*

Edie clicked on the link and read with mounting horror about the awful car crash that had killed the pregnant wife of one of Argentina's top rugby players and left him paralysed from the waist down.

The driver had been Sebastio.

Apparently he'd walked away without a scratch.

The crash had happened just before Christmas almost four years ago. Not long after she'd seen him in that club.

He'd retired from rugby immediately, and the pictures of him from that time showed a man clearly traumatised. In the process of the investigation into the crash it had been discovered that the driver of the other car, who had also died, had had a blood alcohol level three times over the limit.

Sebastio had been cleared of any responsibility. And yet Edie didn't think it was that simple.

There had been moments when she'd seen something dark cross his face. Did this explain his antipathy for the time of year?

There was a link to a video clip, and Edie clicked on it and watched as Sebastio appeared on-screen, looking drawn and haggard. The interview was in Spanish, with subtitles.

Sebastio was saying, 'I was the driver that night and I take full responsibility for what happened—'

'Heard enough?'

Edie almost jumped out of her skin when she registered that the same voice she was listening to was coming from behind her. She quickly shut down the video link and stood up, turning around to see Sebastio leaning against an adjoining door behind her—not the main door.

This door blended into the wall, so he'd had a clear view of what she'd been looking at. She had the vague realisation that this room must adjoin his own private study, which she knew was also on the ground floor.

He was wearing what Edie assumed had been a pristine tuxedo, except now his bow-tie was dangling loose and the top button of his shirt was open. The top few buttons, actually. She could see the dark shadow of chest hair and her breath hitched.

He was holding a heavy crystal glass containing a dark golden liquid and there was a dangerous energy reaching out between them, making her skin prickle. Not with fear. Nothing remotely like that. With awareness. And need. Desperate, awful need.

Her face was so hot she couldn't even pretend to be blasé. All she could do was say, 'I didn't come in here intending to pry—really. I was sending some emails.'

He arched a brow. 'After midnight? That's taking industriousness to a whole new level.'

She ignored his sarcastic tone. 'I couldn't sleep, actually, and I remembered that they should have been sent earlier.'

But as Edie looked at him now she wasn't thinking of her emails. She couldn't get the awful image of the remains of those cars after the crash out of her head. How had he walked away from that? Like some kind of immortal being? And why had he said he was responsible when the other driver had been over the limit?

He pushed himself off the door frame and came into the room. 'You just couldn't help yourself,' he said coldly, stopping a few feet away. 'Everyone wants to know the gory details—even you, apparently.'

Edie was shocked at the bitter cynicism in his voice—and something more indefinable. *Hurt?*

She was about to try and defend herself, but realised she couldn't. She had been prying. Wanting to know more about him.

Her innate sense of honesty forced her to say, 'I'm sorry. I was curious about why you dislike Christmas so much. I shouldn't have been so nosy.'

He made a rude sound and came around in front of the desk. 'Since you're so curious I'll tell you something that no result on a search engine will give you. I hated Christmas long before the accident. I hated Christmas because, apart from a few years in my early childhood, I invariably spent it in the company of nannies. Then, when my parents separated in the most high-profile and bitter divorce Argentina has ever seen, they sent me to boarding school in Switzerland, leaving me there for the entire school year.'

There was a ringing silence after Sebastio stopped speaking. He couldn't believe he'd just let all that tumble out. But anger and a sense of betrayal still pulsed through his body.

He shouldn't be feeling betrayal.

What he did feel was exposed. He'd spent the entire tedious evening cursing himself for not inviting Edie to the dinner party. He'd found himself imagining how she would look in a silky dress rather than paying any attention to his guests' conversation.

And then he'd followed the sound of a noise to find her here, looking at images of his wrecked past. It was as if she'd pulled back the skin on a raw wound.

And yet he was acutely conscious that she was wearing only nightclothes and a thin robe. Her hair was deliciously dishevelled, her eyes heavy-lidded with recent sleep. So maybe she *was* telling the truth…

'I'm sorry, Sebastio… I shouldn't have come down here.'

Her husky voice scraped along his raw nerve-endings. And then he saw it in the depths of her dark blue eyes. Sympathy. Compassion. It rubbed raw against his jangling nerve-endings. Taunting him. Because in spite of everything, and in spite of finding her here like this, he wanted her with a roaring hunger that refused to obey his rational mind.

He needed to take away that sympathy and compassion. He didn't deserve it. He wanted to see something far more explicit and earthy. Desire. The same need that was coursing through his own blood.

With a growing sense of desperation he needed to know that she wanted him too. That he wasn't the only one going slightly crazy. It was the only thing that might soothe the ragged edges of his control.

He closed the distance between them and saw the flare of surprise in her eyes. And yet she didn't move back. She stood her ground. Something inside Sebastio howled with a very male satisfaction.

He moved closer. Until he could smell her unique scent. Delicate, but not flowery. Contradictory. Intriguing. Seductive. Tugging on wispy bits of memory that he couldn't pin down. It made him feel off-balance. As if she knew something he didn't.

Sebastio was in the grip of a hunger and a need he hadn't experienced in a long time. If ever. And it had never felt like this. Raging through his body, incinerating everything in its wake. As if he was being brought painfully back to life.

He had no right being brought back to life. But even that insidious thought couldn't stop him now.

He put down the glass he was holding and reached for her as he said, 'Tell me you want this too…'

Sebastio's hands curled around Edie's arms. She was in shock. Within seconds the tension in the room had changed to a very different kind. The kind of tension that coiled low in her belly and made her skin feel too tight. She couldn't move. She didn't want to move. Sebastio was looking at her with an expression of such raw hunger that she was awed.

*He wanted her.*

A terrifyingly exultant feeling was making her chest expand.

'Edie…?'

He was waiting for her. Edie knew she could step back

from his hands. She knew there were a million and one reasons why it was important not to let Sebastio know how susceptible to him she was. But right now she couldn't think of one.

Shakily she said, 'Yes…'

A look of very male satisfaction crossed Sebastio's face. He lifted a hand and moved it around her neck, holding her. A thumb touched her jaw, tracing its line. Edie had never thought of her jaw as being sensitive before, but a shiver was moving up her body and her skin broke into goosebumps.

He tugged her towards him and they were so close she could feel his body touching hers. She was transfixed by his mouth, the sculpted sensual lines.

His head dipped towards hers, blocking everything out, and then his mouth was on hers, firm and hot and… electrifying.

She'd had a recurring dream for years of what it might have been like if he had kissed her in that club instead of turning her away. But no dream could have possibly come close to this reality.

He pulled her right into him, so that she was flush against his whipcord body. All she was aware of was heat and steely strength. There wasn't a hint of softness anywhere. It didn't intimidate her—it excited her.

She wasn't shutting down now. Far from it. She was blossoming like a flower opening to the heat of the sun.

He drew back. It took an age for Edie to be able to open her eyes, and when she did all she saw were swirling grey pools.

'Let me taste you…'

She wasn't sure what he meant until he put his mouth on hers again and coaxed her to open up, let him in. Sebastio Rivas was an expert. He tipped up her jaw and there was no place she could hide. He explored her with a finesse and a thoroughness that made her dizzy.

Nothing she'd ever experienced could have prepared her for this sensual onslaught. Her legs were weak and she realised she was clutching at his shirt, as if that could stop her from sliding to his feet in a heap. Tentatively she explored him, nipping at his full lower lip, revelling in its fleshy firmness.

He tasted as good as he looked and she wanted more. A lot more. The sensations coursing through her body were overwhelming. She didn't know how to handle it.

And that was when a sliver of cold reality returned to her brain. Reminding her of who she was. Who he was.

She spread her hands on his chest and used all her self-control to push. His mouth lifted from hers and Edie sucked in a shaky breath. She stepped back, out of his embrace, and immediately felt bereft and cold.

'What are we doing?' she asked, her tongue feeling too big for her mouth.

'Proving that you want me.'

Something went cold inside Edie. He hadn't actually said *he* wanted *her*. His eyes glittered and his cheeks were flushed, but that was no comfort. It was triumph. Not desire. She was horrified by how close he'd come to discovering all her deepest secrets and vulnerabilities. Her humiliating inexperience.

Striving to sound as cool and collected as she could, she said, 'This is highly inappropriate. You're my boss.'

He sounded totally nonchalant—as if he hadn't just been setting her on fire and watching her burn. 'Actually, technically, I'm not. You're employed by a subsidiary company of Rivas Bank which has been set up to hire employees in England.'

'I signed a contract to work for *you*.'

He inclined his head. 'Not directly, no. You're actually employed by Azul Incorporated—it's named after an island I own off the coast of Argentina: Santa Azul.'

*He owned an island. Of course he did.*

The gulf between her and this man was laughable. Epic. 'It's still inappropriate,' she said stiffly.

'And you've never done anything inappropriate before?'

Edie's chest tightened. No, she hadn't—because she'd become ill just around the time that all her peers had been testing the boundaries between themselves and their parents. And, in any case, she knew she would never have been the rebellious type.

Her body felt over-sensitised and jittery. Unfulfilled.

And then she saw something alter in Sebastio's demeanour, his expression closing off.

He said coolly, 'Actually you're right. You should go back to bed, Edie.'

*Run along.*

He might not have said those words, but that was what he meant. Edie couldn't believe she'd subjected herself to this again. The arousal in her blood humiliated her. But she rejected the humiliation. Not again.

'What is it? Do you get off on proving that women want you as a punishment for their transgressions?'

He frowned. 'What are you talking about?'

Edie wished she'd just left the room when she had the chance. 'You kissed me because you were angry... You wanted to humiliate me.'

Now his eyes glittered with something far more dangerous. 'You think I kiss women I feel attracted to just to prove a point?'

Edie's heart thudded against her breastbone. 'You mean...?' She couldn't say it.

Sebastio's face was stark. 'That I want you? I thought that was patently obvious.'

Edie felt light-headed. 'I thought you were angry with me.'

'I was…but I still want you. I stopped because if I hadn't we'd be making love on the desk right now, and I don't know if you're ready for that.'

Heat scorched Edie's face.

*Did he know how inexperienced she was? Was it that obvious?*

She was way out of her depth here. And she was a hypocrite. She had to acknowledge that it would have been easier for her to hate Sebastio for humiliating her than deal with the fact that he really did want her.

He was right. She wasn't ready for this.

She stepped back. 'I'm going back to bed. This won't happen again.'

She turned around to leave before she could expose herself any more.

But just before she escaped the room she thought she heard Sebastio's silky voice saying, 'I wouldn't be so sure about that…'

Edie took the stairs to her room two at a time and told herself that by tomorrow morning Sebastio would have put what had happened down to a moment of madness brought on by heightened emotions. And there was no way she was going to expose herself by revealing how cataclysmic his kiss had been.

Sebastio stared into the empty space left behind when Edie had walked out. He could still see the flare of colour on her cheeks and the shocked expression in her eyes.

It had taken all his control to pull back. There'd been

something in her response, though. Untutored. Naive. It had cut through the heat haze in his brain.

She wasn't like the women he normally went for... He grimaced. Or had gone for. Most women, if they sensed his interest, would hurl themselves at him, but she'd held back. And he didn't think it was game-playing—even though he knew he'd be a fool to underestimate any woman.

Sebastio had never underestimated a woman in his life. He'd learnt not to at the hands of his mother, who had used him as a pawn in the bitter feud with his father for years, until she'd realised that his father had long-ago washed his hands of an only son who refused to bend to his will.

And the first woman he'd slept with had taught him his first indelible lesson in choosing lovers when she'd said, 'Women will want you because of your wealth and celebrity. The fact that you're obscenely gorgeous only makes it a sweeter deal for them. Don't ever forget that. As for romance and love? It doesn't exist in our world, darling. Only success and survival.'

And nothing Sebastio had since experienced had done much to change his view.

*Except for Victor and Maya...*

An image of them laughing and dancing at their wedding was vivid, and sharp enough to slice right through Sebastio. He'd destroyed their rare happiness...their lives.

Edie reminded him of Maya. She had the same kind of open and happy demeanour. Not cynical.

A memory flashed back: Maya laughing at him from the back of the car and saying, 'Victor might think you're a lost cause, but I don't. I think there's hope for everyone— even you, Sebastio. Some day you'll meet a woman and she won't fall at your feet in adoration. She'll melt that cynical ice box you call a heart...'

He'd looked at her in the rearview mirror, catching her

sparkling brown eyes, and he'd said, 'Never going to happen, Maya.'

And that was when the world had exploded into a million pieces. Just as he'd been in the middle of affirming his own cynicism to a woman who had exuded nothing but joy and love and openness. He'd killed her. And her baby.

Sebastio broke out of his reverie and his eyes fell on the computer screen, frozen on the image of his haggard face after the accident. He reached over and turned it off, brutally pushing down more memories threatening to resurface.

He was astounded to feel a slight tremor in his hand. He picked up his glass again and downed the remains of his whisky in one go, relishing the burn down his throat. As if it might eclipse the tangled mix of recrimination and desire in his body. It didn't.

All the more reason why he shouldn't pursue Edie.

Sebastio went back into his own study and poured himself another shot of whisky. As he downed it he willed away the potent taste of Edie in his mouth, and the provocative memory of her slender curves pressed against his body. The way her hands had clutched at him so fiercely. And the way she'd opened for him so sweetly.

He cursed. Because all he could think about now was how she might open other parts of herself to him, and how it might feel to sink into that silky embrace and lose himself for ever.

# CHAPTER FOUR

TWO DAYS LATER Edie was feeling edgy. She'd sent Jimmy home and done a quick last-minute check of the grand reception room, where an informal drinks party was taking place that evening.

Sebastio had been in the city for the past two days and nights, but she'd just caught a glimpse of him through the window, emerging from the back of a Jeep. He was dressed in a suit and looking dark and gorgeous against the falling dusk.

And she still couldn't believe he'd kissed her. It felt like a dream.

Matteo appeared in the doorway and Edie flushed to be caught ogling.

'Mr Rivas has sent something to your room for you, Edie.'

'Thank you, Matteo.'

Edie finished her quick check just as the catering staff started to appear for their own preparations.

When she went into her room she saw two boxes sitting on the end of her bed. They were glossy and black. She approached them warily, opening the bigger one first.

It was a dress—satin and teal-green. When she lifted it out of the tissue paper a little sigh of appreciation escaped her mouth. It was a cocktail wrap-dress. Casual, but sexy.

It fell to just below the knee and had a peek-a-boo slit in the back panel.

It was so beautiful. It almost slid out of her hands to the floor it was so slinky. Teal was a colour she'd never have had the nerve to wear.

When she looked in the other box she found nude-coloured strappy high-heeled sandals.

And then she noticed the envelope. She pulled out a thick piece of paper and saw the scrawled writing.

*I'd like you to accept my invitation to the drinks party this evening, Edie.*
*SR*

Edie looked at the note for a long time, as if his handwriting might give her a clue as to what he was up to.

Was this part of a strategy? Seduce her with beautiful clothes that made her sigh and fulfilled her fantasies before telling her he wanted her again? Or kissing her again?

Edie's heart-rate picked up just at the thought. If he kissed her she wouldn't stand a chance. Her brave parting words that it wouldn't happen again would be proved as nothing more than hot air.

*Why are you resisting this?* asked a voice.

Because, she answered herself, she'd developed a strong sense of self-preservation since she'd faced life or death, and everything in her told her that Sebastio Rivas would destroy her if she let him get too close.

*But it would be worth it,* whispered a wicked voice.

Would it, though? Sebastio had no idea how inexperienced she was, and she wasn't about to expose herself any more than she already had. He was hardened, worldly and unmistakably cynical, and she knew enough about his life now to see why.

A man like him wouldn't be gentle or considerate. He didn't really care about Edie. He would take what he wanted and leave her to pick up the pieces.

And yet she couldn't stop an awful feeling of yearning. To go to the party…pretend for a moment that she was like those people. Feel Sebastio's eyes on her…imagine she was the kind of woman who could step up to him and match him.

For a heady moment she allowed herself to imagine a scenario in which she boldly went up to Sebastio and told him she wanted him. In which she allowed him to take her innocence.

Why didn't she take what he was offering? Wouldn't it help her move on with her life?

*No*, Edie told herself, pushing away the illicit daydream. She wasn't ready to bare herself to him and risk his ridicule when he discovered how innocent she was. How truly gauche.

And yet, despite her best intentions, Edie couldn't put the dress down. She went over to the mirror in the dressing room and held it up in front of her body. The teal made her eyes and hair pop dramatically. She could already imagine how it would feel, sliding over her body, and her skin prickled with anticipation.

She cursed Sebastio. But then how could he know how tempting something like this was for someone like her, who had experienced what she had? He must have given hundreds of dresses to hundreds of women.

A sense of fatality washed over her. She knew she didn't have the strength to resist.

Without thinking too deeply about her motives, Edie had a shower and afterwards put on her underwear and tried on the dress. It fit her like a second skin, emphasising curves she hadn't even known she had.

The vee at the front of the dress, where it wrapped around her, dipped down far enough to show more pale skin than Edie had ever shown before.

She pulled the material back to look at the familiar scar just under her right collarbone. It was where the chemo had been administered during her lengthy treatment. It had faded into a fairly innocuous red line, belying the pain and trauma it represented.

Edie quickly pulled the dress over it, not wanting to think about that now.

She noticed that it had got dark outside. She went over to the window and, much like the other evening, saw sleek expensive cars pulling into the courtyard, beautiful people emerging.

Edie's hand tightened on the curtain. What harm would there be if she went to the party? Sebastio was too sophisticated to take her presence as a tacit sign of acquiescence. No doubt he was just toying with her because it amused him. He might want her, but he wasn't about to stake a claim on her in front of his peers!

Sebastio was trying to focus on the conversation he was having with one of Britain's largest hedge fund managers but couldn't stop looking at the door to the room where he was hosting the drinks reception.

*Would she come?*

He'd spent the last two days enduring a series of intense meetings in the city and he'd been uncharacteristically distracted. He couldn't get that kiss with Edie out of his head. It had only stoked his growing hunger.

On a whim, he'd instructed one of his assistants to buy a dress for Edie for the party. Giving in to a fantasy to see her dressed in silk and satin before he'd even decided to invite her to the party. He was losing it.

He felt a prickle of awareness skate over his skin and looked over at the door for the umpteenth time. She was there. His heart skipped a beat. The candlelight made her dress look like liquid silk where it clung to her body. He could see the faint outline of her nipples under the thin material and it was more provocative than the sheerest dress he'd ever seen on a woman.

Her legs were slender and shapely, her feet delicate in the high heels. She looked fresh and beautiful enough to make his blood roar. She also looked endearingly uncertain, hovering in the doorway. And that sent something else entirely through him—something far more dangerous than desire. Because it was emotion.

'Who is that?'

The voice of the man beside him barely impinged on Sebastio's rapidly overheating brain. He said curtly, 'Excuse me.'

He could already see heads swivelling, hear whispers. One man near the door looked as if he was about to approach Edie because she was looking so hesitant, but Sebastio strode towards her, sending silent signals to that man and others to *back off*. He hadn't rugby-tackled anyone in years, but he felt his muscles bunching now, as if in preparation to throw someone aside if they got in his way.

Her hair was a bright shining cap of auburn, and Sebastio realised that in her elegant simplicity she immediately made every other woman in the room look overdone.

He reached her and suddenly felt at an uncharacteristic loss for words.

She gestured to the dress. 'Thank you, but you shouldn't have. I'll pay you back—or clean it so you can return it.'

He dismissed that with a flick of his hand and said, 'It's yours. Please—join us.'

She stepped over the threshold and it felt like a victory

for Sebastio. As if he could sense how close she'd been to not coming.

He'd kissed her and told her he wanted her and yet she'd walked away, telling him it wouldn't happen again. But she was here now. And he still wanted her. It beat through his body like an unstoppable wave of need.

He put a hand to her back, to guide her through the throng, and felt the merest sliver of bare silky skin through the gap in the back of the dress. His brain went white-hot. She tensed under his hand but he propelled her forward, afraid she might still turn tail and run.

He had a vision of sliding his hand all the way in through that tantalising gap and reaching around to cup the pert swell of one—

'Champagne, sir?'

The interruption by the waiter wasn't welcome, but it was necessary. Sebastio took his hand off Edie's back and took two glasses from the tray, handing her one before directing her to a quiet corner.

He tipped his glass to hers. *'Salud.'*

She echoed him, and he watched as she took a sip of the sparkling wine, her nose wrinkling slightly. He'd imagined her like this, against this backdrop, but his imagination had fallen far short of her sheer elegance and classic beauty. Her short hair highlighted her stunning bone structure and the delicate line of her neck and shoulders.

She looked at him and a slight blush was staining her cheeks. She lifted her hand. 'What…? Have I got something on my face?'

He shook his head, marvelling at her lack of awareness even as a far more cynical part of him suspected she had to be playing a part. He'd never wanted a woman as much as he wanted her right now. There were faint warning bells in his head, telling him she must be manipulating him, but he ignored them.

'You're very beautiful,' he said.

She blushed in earnest now. If she *was* acting then she deserved an award. 'I'm not really...but thank you.'

Edie wanted to squirm under Sebastio's intense regard. No man had ever looked at her so closely. She was still trying to get her bearings as the very sleek and beautiful guests around her chatted and sipped expensive wine.

When she'd arrived in the doorway she'd almost turned and run, totally intimidated by the monied crowd. Even though they weren't as formally dressed as the other night, they were still intimidating.

She'd seen Sebastio straight away, standing head and shoulders above everyone else. Not in a tuxedo this time, but no less breathtaking in a three-piece suit.

He'd met her eye, and before she could lose her nerve he'd been cutting a swathe through the crowd to get to her. The sheer force of his charisma had held her motionless, and the next thing he'd been leading her into the crowd, and she'd been trying not to look as self-conscious as she felt.

But she did feel self-conscious. Desperately. As if everyone here could see under the fancy dress and know that she was still inexperienced and awkward.

Why had he asked her here? Because he knew that, in spite of her brave words the other night, she still wanted him with a hunger bordering on desperation? Because he knew she would be easy to seduce?

Just the faintest touch of his hand on the bare skin of her back as he'd propelled her through the crowd had been enough to send her pulse into triple time. She didn't want to look down because she could feel her nipples, tight and hard against the sheer lace of her bra. Were they visible under the thin silk?

Embarrassment rose up in a hot wave. She never should have succumbed to the temptation to put on this dress and attend the party.

She was about to open her mouth and make an excuse when Sebastio said in a low voice, just for her ears, 'I want you, Edie.'

She looked at him. She didn't doubt what he said. It resonated in her body, setting off a chain reaction of sensations. Prickling heat under her skin. Awareness down low in her belly. Damp heat between her legs.

Past and present meshed for a moment, and the humiliation Edie had felt four years ago jarred painfully with Sebastio's declaration now. He sounded so nonchalant, as if he told women all the time that he wanted them. And of course he did! He was a consummate lover. Hadn't she seen him in action four years ago? Surrounded by beauties before kissing one of them and making sure that Edie saw it.

Edie felt more than exposed now. She felt as if he'd reached inside her head, taken out her deepest yearnings and fantasies, and was now teasing her with them. Because he could.

She reacted from that place of hurt and humiliation and said, without thinking, 'Just because you rejected me four years ago, please don't feel like you owe me anything...'

The words were out and hanging between them, and Edie saw Sebastio frowning just as the full realisation hit her of what she'd said. Before she could utter another word, he spoke.

'Rejection? What are you talking about? I didn't even know you four years ago.'

Instant panic flooded Edie and she gabbled, 'It doesn't matter. Forget I said anything.'

She turned to leave but Sebastio caught her arm, restraining her. At the same moment two men came up to them, seeking to speak with Sebastio. His hand tightened on her arm and Sebastio said something to the men that made them step away for a moment. They were looking at Edie curiously and she managed to pull free of Sebastio's hand.

He must have sensed her intention to run as far and as fast as she could. He stood in front of her. Stern. 'Do *not* leave. This conversation is not over, Edie.'

*Oh, yes, it is*, she thought to herself.

'Forget I said anything—it was nonsense.'

She backed away and Sebastio frowned again, saying warningly, 'Edie...'

Before he could touch her again Edie turned and fled, putting her glass of champagne down on a table as she left. She walked blindly across the reception hall and found herself in the main library, with its floor-to-ceiling shelves and its smell of old leather. A curiously comforting smell.

She walked over to a window and wrapped her arms around herself. Big fat snowflakes were falling outside, but that fact barely registered on her consciousness.

Her heart was pounding and she thought, *What have I done?* The last thing she'd wanted to do was draw Sebastio's attention to the fact that they'd met before. It was excruciating.

She'd never expected to see him again, and she'd certainly never expected to be in a situation where she did meet him again and there was this explosive chemistry between them. It had been so close to her fantasies that she'd automatically assumed he was privy to them on some level. That he was using that knowledge to tease her because he couldn't possibly really want her.

But of course he couldn't know her secret fantasies. And all she'd done was expose herself spectacularly.

*That kiss the other night hadn't felt like a fantasy. It had felt all too real.* Edie quivered just thinking about it.

She heard some movement coming from the main hall, but was too afraid of seeing Sebastio to go outside and investigate what was happening. So she hid in the library and told herself that she would return to her flat in Islington in the morning. There would be no need for her to stay the weekend. She and Jimmy would have plenty of time to redress the house in time for the next party early next week.

She needed to get away from the disturbing orbit of Sebastio's presence before he saw through her completely and realised how utterly flimsy her defences were. She might have fantasised about being a match for him, but she knew she wasn't.

Sebastio's jaw was tight with irritation and frustration. He'd just seen off the last of his guests and was standing outside Edie's bedroom door, yanking open his tie and loosening his shirt.

It didn't help.

He couldn't believe she'd just slipped out of that room with a flash of green silk, like some ethereal sprite. He couldn't believe she'd defied him. But then she'd consistently confounded his expectations since he'd met her.

He knocked on the door and waited. No sound. His frustration levels increased. He opened the door, saying, 'Edie…' But the room was in darkness. She couldn't be asleep already. He flicked on the light and saw the bed was neatly made up, and empty.

He cursed and closed the door. He went back downstairs and passed Matteo, who was busy organising getting all the temporary staff home. When Sebastio asked him if he'd seen Edie he mentioned the library.

Sebastio knew before he'd even stepped over the threshold that she was there. He felt the familiar prickling awareness over his skin. He walked into the dimly lit room and saw her. Her back was to him and she was looking out of the window. She looked incredibly slender, and something tugged on his memories, but it was too fleeting and vague to hold on to.

*'Just because you rejected me four years ago...'*

Sebastio closed the door behind him and saw her tense when she heard the sound. She turned around slowly.

He folded his arms. 'So, are you going to explain what you meant by that comment?'

He'd tracked her down. In spite of the vast space of the room, and the house around them, Edie had never felt more claustrophobic.

'You shouldn't leave your guests alone.'

'They've all left.'

Edie frowned. 'But it can't be nine o'clock yet.'

'Look outside.'

'I… I was…' She turned around again and gasped.

The world had turned white within minutes and the snowflakes were coming thick and fast. She shivered, even though she couldn't feel the cold.

Sebastio stood beside her. 'The weather office issued an emergency alert. The blizzard-like conditions they forecast for the weekend are hitting sooner than predicted. We felt it would be prudent to warn our guests so they could get home in time.'

Edie hadn't even been aware of a weather alert. The house was like a luxurious cocoon.

'Do you want a drink?'

Edie turned to see Sebastio go over to a drinks cabinet. He took a crystal stopper out of a bottle and poured himself a measure of dark golden liquid.

She shook her head. 'No, thank you.'

She wanted to leave, like those guests. But her feet were

rooted to the spot. She was unable to take her eyes off the fluid movement of Sebastio's body as he lifted the small glass and took a sip. His tie was undone and the top buttons of his shirt were open.

He came back over to where she was standing. 'Well, Edie? What did you mean by what you said? Have we met before?'

Edie gulped and regretted not asking for a drink. She forced her gaze up to Sebastio's. She couldn't lie. He'd see through it in an instant. 'Yes. We did meet. Briefly.'

His mouth tightened. 'Yet apparently long enough for me to reject you?'

Edie wanted a hole to appear in the floor and swallow her whole. She paced away from Sebastio, unable to keep still.

Then she stopped and faced him. 'It was at a nightclub in Edinburgh, four years ago. You'd just played a rugby match against Scotland.'

He frowned. 'Yes… I remember that match. It was our last away match before—' He stopped abruptly. His gaze narrowed on her. 'What happened?'

Edie wondered if he'd been about to say that it had been their last match before the accident. The timing would be right.

She felt silly now, when she thought of the crash. Her encounter with him had been such a small event and yet it had had huge repercussions for her. How could she explain that?

'I just…saw you. And I wanted to…to meet you.' She cringed inwardly. This was so much worse than she had imagined. 'I tried to talk to you and you told me to leave you alone.'

*More or less.*

Sebastio's skin felt too tight. As he looked at Edie he realised that the wispy sense of déjà-vu had been real. He *had* seen her before. He remembered her huge eyes looking at him with such a sense of naked hope that they'd sliced right through him. Now she looked at him far more warily. Had he done that? Or someone else?

Except… 'You looked different then…'

She seemed to go paler in the dim light. 'You can't possibly remember.'

But he hardly heard her as he pieced the event together. 'You were a very young girl.'

'I was nineteen,' Edie said, almost defensively.

Sebastio looked at her. 'Like I said, very young. Fragile. Big eyes. And your hair was longer…'

Edie touched her hair self-consciously, surprised he'd recalled that detail of her wig.

'Why didn't you tell me when we met again?'

Edie's hand dropped from her hair. She avoided his eye. 'I was embarrassed. I approached you and you basically told me to *run along*. And then you kissed a woman in front of me.'

'That wasn't very nice of me.'

Edie made a small shrugging movement. 'I'd disturbed you with your friends.'

Sebastio recalled the incident now—it had stuck in his mind for days afterwards. Her eyes had been so huge, and full of a kind of hope and innocence he'd never really seen before. That was why he'd sent her away, even though something about her had been very compelling.

He recalled now that she'd made him feel jaded. And restless.

He touched her jaw, tracing the feminine line. 'I'm sorry I was harsh, Edie, but believe me I did you a favour that night. I was a different person then…you would have liked me even less than you do now.'

He had told himself at the time that he'd done it because

he hadn't wanted to taint her with his cynicism, but he realised now it had been for far more complex and personal
reasons. It was as if those huge eyes had seen right through
him to the root of his sense of dissatisfaction.

And she still had that ability. Except now he couldn't
push her away. He wanted her too much.

'I don't *not* like you, Sebastio. I just never expected to
meet you again.'

'And yet here we are.'

Sebastio tipped up Edie's chin with a finger as lust coiled
tight inside him. It would appear that he had no such qualms
about not tainting her with his cynicism now.

'Maybe you like me a little... Is that what you're saying?'

'Are you telling me you really care what I think about
you?'

Her eyes flashed with dark blue fire. She might have
projected fragility and innocence four years ago, and sometimes she still did, but she'd obviously grown up too. A part
of Sebastio lamented the loss of some of that innocence.
Which was ridiculous.

He was surprised by an urge to tell her that *yes*, he did
actually care. When he shouldn't. This was about sex. Not
feelings.

'We don't need to care about each other to want each
other.'

*Wow.* Edie absorbed this. She couldn't fault him for not
being brutally honest. She felt a dart of hurt but pushed
it aside. She pulled her head back, dislodging his finger
from her chin.

'Edie...let me be very clear. What I want from you is
purely physical. I don't do relationships. I don't offer commitment. I'm not kind or understanding. I want you...and
what I'm offering is a finite affair until such time as this

thing between us burns out. But don't ever expect anything more, because I can't give it and you'll get hurt.'

Edie wanted to prick the arrogant well-worn cynicism he wore so well. 'You're saying you've never been hurt?'

He shook his head and a hard expression settled over his features. 'Let's just say I learnt at an early age not to expect too much.'

'How do you know I haven't learnt the same?' Edie riposted.

Sebastio reached out again and trailed a finger across her jaw. Her breath hitched.

'Because I can see it in your eyes, Edie. That's not a bad thing. It's just not for me.'

Edie felt foolish for trying to prove something to him. He was right. She would ultimately expect something more and that would be emotional suicide with a man like this.

His finger was trailing down from her jaw to her neck and he rested it on her pulse-point. She could feel the blood pulsing against the slight pressure he was exerting.

'I want you, Edie. More than I've wanted a woman for a long time. I propose that we explore this mutual chemistry until it burns itself out.'

*Until it burns itself out.*

Edie shivered with awareness. That knot of tension tightened in her belly. She looked up at him, as if she might find the answers to questions she didn't even know she was asking written in his features or in those impenetrable grey eyes.

She'd always wanted to find someone she could connect with on a deep level. Not just a physical one.

As much as her parents had smothered her, she'd always envied their strong and supportive bond. Yet in spite of their bond, and their love for her, she'd never felt as isolated as she had during her cancer treatment.

She'd felt if she was behind a glass wall, looking out, unable to connect with anyone, having no one with whom she could share the depth of her fears and anguish. She'd always longed to feel a sense of connection that would eclipse that awful sense of isolation.

And she had felt it that night in that club. When her eyes had locked with Sebastio's. As improbable as it might have been. With one glance it had been as if Edie had known on some deep and instinctive level that Sebastio could understand and empathise with her sense of isolation, and she'd felt connected to someone else for the first time in a long time.

And here she was, standing in front of him again with that sense of connection surging through her blood. Obliterating all the reasons why she shouldn't be tempted by him.

Because indulging in an affair with Sebastio Rivas would come at a cost.

What Sebastio was offering was anathema to her, because she knew she craved a deep and lasting connection with a man.

And yet she ached for him. Only him. Even though he was only offering her this. A moment out of time.

The last thing she should be doing was thinking of saying yes, but it beat through her body like an inexorable wave. *Yes, yes, yes.*

This man had spurned her gauche advances once, but he'd set the bar so high that she'd never allowed another man to get close. She had a chance here to rewrite history. To fulfil the fantasy she'd had in her head since that night. That he hadn't turned her away.

Was she going to remain a virgin for ever? Maybe she needed this to move on with her life?

Doubt entered her mind then. Was she crazy to be contemplating this? If he discovered she was a virgin he'd run a mile. It was on the tip of her tongue to tell him…but something was stopping her. Something illicit and rebellious.

She wanted this. Even if it was for only one night. She would worry about the repercussions later.

'Edie…?'

Sebastio's voice cut through the maelstrom in her head. Edie shut it out. She obeyed the beat in her blood and took a giant leap into the unknown.

'Yes… I want you, Sebastio.'

Sebastio heard Edie's words but it took a second for them to sink in. Any kind of finesse he might have had before seemed to have deserted him. His blood surged and he stepped forward, cupping Edie's jaw, stroking his thumb across silky skin, feeling the hectic pulse against his hand.

'Are you sure about this?'

She nodded, biting her lip. Her vivid blue gaze dropped to his mouth and Sebastio couldn't wait any longer. He had to taste her again. *Now.*

He walked her back until she hit a wall of books. He had to put his hands on the shelves either side of her head, because he wasn't sure if he could control himself if he touched her.

He dipped his head towards hers and for an infinitesimal moment let his mouth hover above hers. Her scent wound around him, sweet and fresh. He had the strangest sensation that he was tipping over the edge of something he'd never encountered before but he pushed it out of his head, telling himself it was just the edge of his control…

Edie's breath had deserted her altogether as she'd waited for that first exquisite touch of Sebastio's mouth on hers. And when it came she nearly slid down the shelves at her back. Instant heat flooded her whole body and she reached out to clutch at his clothes in a bid to stay standing.

The kiss burnt any lingering doubts from Edie's mind.

How on earth had she thought this was a choice? This was a *need*. And she knew she'd never need like this again. It was bittersweet to be already lamenting the absence of Sebastio's touch even as he was kissing her.

Her hands clutched at him tighter as a kind of desperation wound through her. And finally he brought his hands down and cupped her face, angling her head so his kiss could go even deeper.

Edie was vaguely aware of the shelves of books at her back. Her brain was fusing with white heat. Sebastio's mouth left hers and she sucked in a deep, shuddering breath. He trailed kisses across her jaw and down her neck and her head fell back, too heavy to hold up.

Sebastio smoothed a hand across her hip and her behind, cupping her bottom through the thin, slippery material of her dress. The pulse jumped between her legs, making her aware of the damp heat signalling her intense desire.

Edie's hands climbed Sebastio's chest, exploring the strong contours and the breadth of his shoulders. He was so big, but she didn't feel overwhelmed or scared. She wanted more.

'Sebastio…please…' She didn't even realise she'd spoken out loud until he drew back, eyes glittering fiercely.

'What…?'

Edie didn't know how to articulate what she wanted, so she just reached up and pressed her mouth to his again. He seemed to hesitate a moment, and then he gathered her to him so that her whole body was pressed against his. Her breasts were crushed against his chest. His erection was digging into her belly. He felt impossibly big, and hard, and acting on blind instinct, Edie cupped him through his trousers.

He hissed a breath through his teeth, and then said roughly, 'You— I want to see you.'

Her hand fell away as Sebastio tugged on the knot at her waist, causing her dress to fall open. She barely felt the tiny draught skate over her hot skin. Sebastio pushed the dress apart and put his hands on her bare waist, spanning it easily.

'Beautiful… Edie. You're beautiful.'

She couldn't even duck her head to hide away from the compliment. She felt drunk. Sebastio brought up a hand and expertly flicked open her bra at the front. Then he smoothed it back and placed his whole hand on one breast.

Edie nearly cried out. Her nipple was so tight it hurt, and it scraped against his palm with a delicious friction. He bent his head and flicked a tongue across the tip, and Edie pressed her thighs together to try and stem the spasm of desire as Sebastio's mouth closed over her nipple and he sucked roughly.

Her hands were in his hair, and she had to be hurting him, but she was only aware of the exquisite drugging, dragging pleasure of his mouth on her breasts. First one and then the other.

Things seemed to escalate within seconds. Edie was panting, her hand seeking Sebastio's body again, fingers fumbling with his trousers. She wanted to take him in her hand, feel that potent hardness.

He said something guttural in Spanish—something she couldn't understand. And then her hands were being gently pushed aside as he undid his belt and trousers. Edie looked at Sebastio through a haze of lust. His hair was flopping over his forehead and his face was flushed. He took her breath away.

Then she looked down and saw him take himself in his hand. Her mouth dried. He was big. And thick and hard. She saw moisture glistening at the head.

Edie felt a moment of trepidation as Sebastio's hands came to her panties and he pulled them down over her hips. They fell on the floor at her feet. She was bared to him completely now, her dress wide open, but she couldn't seem to drum up any self-consciousness, even though he was the first man to see her all but totally naked. She only felt a fierce desire to fuse with him.

He looked at her for a long moment and then pressed close. She felt him against her bare skin. With his other hand he reached between her legs and Edie's whole body went taut as he dragged a finger along the seam of her body, opening her up before sinking inside her.

She thought she might have screamed. She bent her head into Sebastio's shoulder as his finger moved in and out, releasing her desire and making the tension deep inside her coil so tightly that she wasn't sure where it could go—until it exploded and she tensed against his hand, her whole being pulsating on waves of pleasure so intense that she almost lost consciousness for a moment.

After a couple of seconds Sebastio lifted one of Edie's legs and held it, aligning their bodies until the tip of his penis was touching her core. Little after-shocks of pleasure were still coursing through her system but she felt herself moving to accomodate his body, anticipating the moment when he would surge between her legs, stretching her wide. Filling her. She ached for it. As if she'd been waiting for this all her life.

But for a second he stopped. And in that moment, a sliver of sanity returned to Edie's overheated brain. She was about to be made love to for the first time, standing up against a bookshelf. And suddenly the prospect of Sebastio's reaction when he realised she was a virgin made her go cold.

She could feel his muscles bunching as he prepared to join their bodies and she put a hand on his chest. It was trembling. She realised very belatedly that he was still almost fully dressed.

'Wait…' Her voice sounded scratchy.

Immediately he stopped and looked at her. 'Okay?'

Edie shook her head.

Sebastio put down her leg and pulled back. 'What is it?'

Edie reached for one side of her dress and pulled it over herself. Now she felt self-conscious. 'There's something I should tell you…before we go further.'

'Edie…?'

She forced herself to look at him. 'I haven't…done this before.'

He looked confused, and then she could see realisation dawning. 'You mean you've never—'

'Had sex. Yes.' She rushed to finish for him before he could say it out loud.

The air between them seemed to cool almost immediately. Sebastio drew back and did up his trousers. Edie pulled her dress together, feeling completely undone.

'Why didn't you tell me before?'

Sebastio's voice skated like an arctic wind over her skin. She secured the fastening on her dress after a few fumbled attempts. Her bra was still open and her bare nipples were sensitive against the thin silk. She saw her panties on the floor and bent down to pick them up.

Her whole body was screaming for fulfilment. But she was glad she'd stopped Sebastio because if his reaction now was anything to go by it would have been ten times worse if she'd said nothing.

'I didn't expect this to happen…here. Like this.'

Edie's words scored into Sebastio's skin like barbs. He reeled at this information. Edie was a virgin. Innocent. Still innocent. And he'd been about to take her like some out-of-control teenager with his first woman. He'd never lost it with a woman like that. *Ever*.

Caustic words spilled out before he could stop them,

self-recrimination bubbling over. 'So you wouldn't have stopped me if we'd been in a bedroom? Is that what you're saying?' He cursed in Spanish. And then, 'Dammit, Edie… I could have hurt you.'

Actually he knew he *would* have hurt her. He had been close to losing his reason at the mere touch of her hot, damp sex against his erection.

In the dim light of the room, with her hair dishevelled and her dress crumpled around her, she looked sinfully sexy but also impossibly fragile. He had a flashback to that nightclub in Edinburgh. It was all so clear now. She'd been infinitely more fragile then, but she was the same person. *Still innocent.*

The fact that he'd met her before…and she'd known all this time while he hadn't…made Sebastio feel doubly exposed now.

Maybe it was also because she was linking him back to a time in his life that he didn't want to think about. The time after the crash, when he'd blocked everything out. Cut himself off from the rugby world and his friends.

Edie was looking at him and her expression was all at once vulnerable and defiant. He might not have known her consciously when they'd met again, but deep down he'd known her.

He denied what his body was screaming for—fulfilment. His wounds were too raw and close to the surface. He shook his head. 'I don't do this, Edie. I don't initiate innocents.'

He saw how she flinched slightly but he welcomed it. She had to know the type of man he was. If he had a tiny modicum of humanity left—one small piece of his soul that wasn't toxic and guilt-ridden—then this was it. He refused to be the one to take Edie's innocence. He didn't deserve it.

# CHAPTER FIVE

*I DON'T INITIATE INNOCENTS.*

Edie just wanted to leave. With as much dignity as she could muster. Whatever had happened before with this man paled into insignificance next to this new and fresh humiliation.

She managed to say as coolly as she could, 'I think I'll go to my room now.'

She prayed her legs wouldn't wobble as she stepped around Sebastio to walk out of the room. The fact that he was barely dishevelled was even more galling. She'd practically been naked while he'd maintained control at all times. Did the man ever lose it?

Edie had a sudden and very uncharacteristic urge to see Sebastio lose control some time. Anything to make her feel less ragged.

She was almost at the door when he said from behind her, 'Edie…'

Reluctantly she turned around. He'd never looked more tall or forbidding against the timeless backdrop of the room.

He said, 'I don't mean to be harsh, but I won't be the one to take your innocence from you. I won't have that on my conscience too.'

Edie heard his words. Barely. She was too eager to leave. But what she understood in that moment was that he was effectively saying, *It's not you, it's me.* Which made it even worse.

'You don't have to explain, Sebastio.'

When she got back to her room she let the dress fall to the floor and stripped off her bra and panties. After a steaming hot shower she crawled into bed and willed sleep to come and obliterate everything. Especially how she could have done this to herself again. With the same man.

When Edie was up and dressed the next morning she packed her small suitcase for the weekend with every intention of going back to her flat.

When she got to the main hall, though, she heard a familiar voice say, 'Where are you going?'

Hoping that nothing of the previous evening's humiliation would show on her face, Edie turned around—and nearly fell over. Sebastio was standing at the bottom of the stairs in faded jeans and a long-sleeved woollen jumper. His hair was dark and messy. Jaw stubbled. He looked thoroughly disreputable and more gorgeous than ever.

Edie's insides twisted. She was doing the right thing. Going home. There was only one more event and then she would be free to get on with her life and forget about Sebastio Rivas for ever.

'I'm going home for the weekend.'

He shook his head as he came towards her. 'No, you're not.'

Indignation and panic raced up Edie's spine. 'You can't force me to stay here.'

He looked grim as he walked past her to the main door. 'It's not me stopping you from leaving—it's the weather.'

He opened the wide front door and Edie felt an icy blast of air as she looked out in shock to see that overnight the world had turned completely white. She approached the door after putting her suitcase down. There were drifts of snow almost as high as the steps leading up to the house. The weather warning he'd told her about.

'Even if you could get out of the estate, there's no public transport running.'

'So what does this mean?' she asked redundantly.

'It means that we're snowed in for the forseeable future.'

By that evening Sebastio's whole body was on edge with a mixture of sexual frustration and something that felt bizarrely like...*concern*. He hadn't seen Edie all day. She'd done a good job of avoiding him. And could he blame her?

Since she'd told him about their meeting in the nightclub he hadn't been able to stop thinking about it. That night had always been so clear in his mind.

It had been a week before the tragic car crash. Victor hadn't come out to the nightclub with them after the match, preferring to stay in the hotel to video call Maya. Sebastio could remember an awful feeling of envy mixed with resentment that his friend's life had changed so much.

Since Victor had fallen in love and married, Sebastio had felt increasingly dissatisfied. As if just the existence of Victor and Maya's relationship had thrown all that was lacking in his own life into sharp relief. Which was crazy, because he'd never been under any illusion about wanting to settle down and have babies. And yet, if the complex feelings his friends' relationship had evoked within him were any indication, apparently his true desires lay in another direction entirely. One which could not exist for someone as cynical and jaded as Sebastio.

He remembered how on edge he'd felt that night in the club. When Edie had approached him, with her big eyes and her naked expression of hope, it had jarred too painfully. Reminding him of the fact that he envied his friend while at the same time rejecting every possibility that he could want the same thing. Because if he admitted that then he'd be admitting he was weak. Not strong.

He'd taken a woman into his bed that night in a bid to try and restore some sense of equilibrium, but he hadn't been able to get Edie's huge dark blue eyes out of his head. She'd haunted him.

Sebastio saw his reflection in the window of his study now, highlighted against the blackness outside. Not for the first time he wished that his face was criss-crossed with scars. Wished for some kind of physical proof that he had destroyed lives. If he was physically scarred then it would be like a warning to people—*to Edie*—to stay away. A physical reminder that his cynicism had destroyed something very pure and that he could not be trusted not to cause hurt.

He couldn't even feel much satisfaction that he'd done the noble thing by telling her he wouldn't take her innocence. He couldn't feel noble when his body still burned, and when he knew he'd done it as much to protect himself as to protect her. She came too close to that place inside him that was still raw with regret, guilt and grief.

Edie was sweating, and her lungs felt as if they were about to explode, but she launched another high kick at the punching bag and welcomed the burn. Anything to try and eclipse that other burn inside her. The one she felt for Sebastio. The one she feared she'd never *un*-feel again.

As the day had worn on, Edie's sense of humiliation had faded to be replaced with anger. At herself. And at Sebastio. How dared he decide on her behalf not to seduce her? As if he was doing her a favour?

His words had reverberated in her head all day.

*'I won't be the one to take your innocence from you. I won't have that on my conscience too.'*

What had he meant by that? It sounded as if he was referring to a sense of guilt. Guilt about the accident? She remembered the video clip—Sebastio saying that he was responsible for the accident...

Edie had lost any sense of propriety over her own body during her illness, when she'd been poked and prodded and filled with toxic but ultimately life-saving chemicals. She'd vowed never to let herself feel so out of control of it again.

She stopped kicking the punching bag for a moment, sweat dripping into her eyes as she absorbed that thought. She knew what was good for her body. And Sebastio was good for her body. She'd never felt so alive as she had last night in his arms. With his mouth on hers. *On her breasts.* His hand between her legs.

She ached for the fulfilment she instinctively knew only he could give her.

She didn't regret telling him she was a virgin, but she regretted him stopping. He hadn't stopped because he'd been turned off by her innocence. He'd stopped because of some kind of moral reasoning. Which incensed Edie now. It was as if he'd decided she wasn't robust enough to handle him.

She wiped her face with a damp towel, her heart thudding with adrenaline as much as exertion. She wanted Sebastio Rivas. But was she willing to put herself on the line one more time?

When she'd been ill she'd believed she was going to die. It had only been when she'd started responding to treatment that she'd believed in another possibility.

Since she'd received the all-clear she'd been determined to make the most of her life. And yet she knew that some things still held her back. Little things—like the fear of letting her hair grow long again in case the illness returned. And a fear of intimacy because she'd missed out on that period of her life where she would have explored it naturally.

And then she'd met Sebastio Rivas four years ago and no man had come close to him since.

And now, amazingly, she'd met him again and he wanted her. This was an opportunity to move on with her life. To seize back control. Karma. The scenario she'd imagined the other evening—seducing Sebastio—suddenly didn't seem so ridiculous.

With a sense of growing determination Edie went upstairs from the basement. It was dark outside. The snow had stopped falling. There wasn't a sound. There was something otherworldly about knowing that they were completely cocooned, as if normal service had been interrupted. As if she could do anything.

Edie knew there was no way she'd have the nerve to do what she was about to do under normal circumstances.

She went into the library—the scene of last night's humiliation. She didn't look at where she'd been pressed against the shelves by his big body. Where her dress had been open and she'd pushed herself wantonly against his hand.

She went straight over to the drinks table and poured herself a shot of whisky, drinking it down in one go. The warmth slipped down her throat and sank into her stomach. Spreading outwards. Infusing her with a sense of confidence that she could do this.

Instinctively she seemed to know that Sebastio would be in his study—and, sure enough, when she stood outside the door she heard the low rumble of his voice on the other side. He was speaking in Spanish.

Without waiting for her nerves or a sense of rationality to kick in, Edie knocked on the door and went in.

* * *

Sebastio heard the sound and looked up from the tediously boring phone call to see Edie standing in the doorway to his study. His brain went completely blank for a long moment as he absorbed the fact that she was wearing tight-fitting Lycra jogging pants and a cropped vest top. Her hair was damp and her pale skin was glowing from exertion. She had a towel draped around her neck.

Sebastio had put the phone down before he even realised that he hadn't ended the conversation. All he could see were her slender curves and those huge eyes. For a moment he wondered if he was going mad—conjuring her up.

'I have something to say.'

*She wasn't a hallucination.*

Sebastio stood up. He put out a hand. 'Please, come in.'

She walked in and he caught her scent—musky. She'd obviously just been in the gym. He imagined how her skin must be warm and damp, as it would be after sex. Blood rushed south, emptying his head.

She stopped in front of his desk. Her face was set with an expression of determination and something else, something more vulnerable. He could feel the control he'd had to exert since last night fraying.

It made his voice curt. 'What did you want to say?'

Edie almost lost her nerve then. Sebastio looked so remote. Formidable. She wondered if she'd dreamt up what had happened in the library. But, no…she could see it in his eyes. The glitter of heat. Banked. But there.

She swallowed. 'I want you to make love to me.'

A muscle pulsed in his jaw. 'I already told you, Edie. I won't do it.'

Suddenly he'd discovered a noble conscience? Edie wanted to growl with frustration and remind him that he had a reputation as an international playboy.

'Because you don't want the responsibility?' she asked. 'Because I'm a virgin?'

He put his hands on the table. He looked fierce. 'There's more to it than that.'

'Your sense of guilt? And some misplaced notion that taking my innocence will add to that guilt?'

He went very still. 'What are you talking about?'

Edie mustered up all her courage and wished she'd taken another whisky when she'd had the chance. 'You said in the video that you took responsibility for the car crash, so you obviously feel guilty about what happened to your friends.'

Sebastio's voice was arctic. 'That is none of your business.'

A lesser woman than Edie might have quailed and run by now, but she'd gone too far. She had nothing to lose.

She pointed at herself. '*I* take full responsibility for my actions. If I want to let you take my virginity then that's my choice. There will be no guilt involved. Maybe you think that because I'm inexperienced I won't be able to handle an affair, but, the way I see it, my inexperience is only a very minor physical fact.'

'It's more than a minor physical fact, Edie. Emotionally—'

She put up a hand. 'I can handle my own emotions.'

Now he looked grim. 'I'm not negotiating this, Edie. I refuse to be the one to take your innocence.'

Not knowing where she was getting the nerve to do this, Edie said tauntingly, 'You don't want me enough—is that it? Maybe my virginity is a turn-off?'

'Edie...' he said warningly.

She backed away from the desk, feeling a cool chill skate over her skin. Her confidence was draining rapidly. She'd underestimated Sebastio. And maybe she'd overestimated his desire for her.

'Don't worry about it, Sebastio,' she said as loftily as she could. 'I'm sure I'll find someone who does want me enough.'

She turned to walk out, but just as she was about to put her hand on the door she heard an indistinct statement that sounded like *No way*.

It all happened so fast she lost her breath. Sebastio had slammed the door closed before she could open it, put his hands on her shoulders, turned her around and was glaring down into her face with an expression of intensity she'd never seen before.

'What the hell is that supposed to mean? *"Find someone who does want me enough"*?'

Edie looked up at him in awe. He was all coiled, taut energy, and for a second she felt sorry for the opponents he must have encountered on the rugby pitch.

She fought not to let him intimidate her. She lifted her chin. 'Just that… If you don't want me then I'm sure someone else will.'

He growled. 'Not *want* you? You're the first woman I've wanted in four years. I want you so much I can still taste you in my mouth. Damn you.'

And suddenly need met heat and he was kissing her with ruthless precision. The first thing that swept through her system was relief. It had worked. Her very naive attempt to goad him into action had worked.

And then she thought of what he'd just said and pulled her head back, breathing hard. 'What do you mean, the first woman in four years?'

Sebastio caged her in with his hands on the door behind her. He looked at her. 'I haven't had a lover in four years.'

He obviously didn't relish admitting that, if the bite in his voice was anything to go by.

*Since the accident.* She didn't say it. She thought it.

That revelation made something very fluttery erupt in Edie's abdomen but she had to ignore it and remind herself that he was just talking about *sex*. Not emotions, just sex. Nevertheless, the fluttery feeling wouldn't go away.

He said, 'It's been a while, Edie. I don't want to hurt you.'

She shook her head, slightly awed by the look in his eyes, it was so penetrating and intense. 'You won't. I'm sure of it.'

*Not physically, anyway.*

She put her hands on his chest and moved them up to his shoulders. She felt the bunched strength of his muscles and her insides clenched.

Sebastio looked down into Edie's face. He could see the determination in her eyes. The firm set of her chin. And acres of tantalising pale flesh. The pert swells of her breasts under the stretchy material of her top. The gentle flare of her hips. Slim thighs. And he wanted her. More than anything he'd ever wanted.

'Are you sure about this?'

She nodded. 'Yes.' There was no hesitation.

The anticipation that surged in Sebastio's blood eclipsed any lingering doubt. He couldn't turn away from this now if wild horses were trying to stop him.

He took Edie's hand, wordlessly leading her from his study through the silent hall, and up the stairs to the bedrooms.

Edie felt the barest sliver of trepidation as Sebastio opened his bedroom door and led her in. She had an impression of a very sparsely furnished room in comparison to her bedroom and the other rooms in the house. Almost ascetic. But that was soon forgotten when he took her over to the massive bed and turned to face her, dropping her hand.

The air was thick between them. So thick Edie could

hardly breathe. Her heart was pumping. She wished for a second she'd been less impulsive. She was wearing sweats! She wished she was in the gorgeous green silk dress. But it was too late.

Sebastio was reaching for her, putting his hands on her waist and pulling her to him. All she could feel was heat and steel, and all she could smell was his uniquely masculine scent. Musky and woody.

His hands traced her waist and a ball of tension lodged deep in her core. She sucked in a breath as he trailed the backs of his hands across her bare belly.

He said, 'I want to see you.'

Edie nodded her head jerkily, biting her lip as Sebastio's big hands came to the front fastening of her cropped top. It opened and he pushed it aside, over her shoulders and down her arms so it fell to the floor.

She was naked from the waist up, and in spite of all her bravado she suddenly felt shy.

He tipped her chin up and she looked at him. 'Okay?'

Something about his concern unknotted something inside her and she nodded. 'I want to see you too.'

His mouth tipped up ever so slightly at one side, and with a graceful economy of movement he lifted up his top and pulled it off, revealing a broad muscular chest. Not an ounce of fat. Defined pectoral muscles covered in dark curling hair led down to a taut belly, dissected by a line of dark hair that disappeared under his jeans.

Edie forgot about feeling shy. She reached out and smoothed her hands across his chest. Her hands shook a little as she touched him reverently.

Sebastio was afraid he might explode before he'd even get Edie under him on the bed. The way she was looking at him and touching him was seriously heady.

He'd never seen her eyes so big. His gaze dropped and

he took in the provocative view of her breasts. High and firm and fuller than her figure indicated. Small pink nipples. He couldn't resist. He reached out and cupped her breast, running his thumb back and forth across one hard tip, watching how the skin puckered.

He felt the delicate shiver move through her body and his pulse jumped. She was so reponsive.

The edge of the bed was at the back of his legs and he sank down on the side, drawing Edie in between his thighs. He moved his hands around to cup her behind.

Her breasts were at exactly the right height and he drew one small hard nipple into his mouth, suckled and teased before tasting the other one. Edie's hands fisted painfully in his hair, but he didn't even notice the sharp pain…he was gorging himself on Edie's sweet flesh.

Edie was being tortured, but it was a kind of sensual torture she'd never experienced before. Exqusite pain… delicious pain. The flick of Sebastio's tongue across her nipple nearly sent her into orbit. The only thing stopping her from falling down was his legs pressing against hers, trapping her. She never wanted to be set free.

But then he shifted, and Edie slid down to sit on his lap, feeling dazed. Her breasts were throbbing and he cupped one, rubbing a thumb back and forth over one sensitive peak.

Any hopes and dreams she'd had of making love for the first time with someone kind and gentle had been blown out of the water. She'd had no idea that she'd connect on such a primal level with a man who embodied such pure masculine strength and perfection.

How could she have not wanted this inferno of desire? The thought that she might never have known this depth of need and sensation made her feel curiously emotional.

Sebastio asked again, 'Okay?'

Edie hurriedly nodded and blinked rapidly, praying he wouldn't see anything of the emotion in her eyes. 'I'm fine…more than fine.'

Sebastio kissed her again. It was long and luxurious, letting her get her bearings while also ratcheting up the tension coiling tight inside her. When she squirmed on his lap, wanting, *needing* more, Sebastio urged her up so she was standing before him again.

He slowly peeled her leggings down, over her hips and down her legs. She kicked off her sneakers. Now she wore only her panties.

He stood up and snapped open the button on his jeans before pushing them down and off, taking his underwear with them. Edie couldn't breathe. He was naked. And massively aroused.

If she'd had any sliver of doubt that he wanted her it was gone.

'Your underwear—take it off.' He sounded hoarse.

Edie tugged down her panties too. She held her breath, suddenly very aware that perhaps he was used to women who were more…groomed. But she sneaked a glance and the way he was looking at her… She could see a flare of colour across his cheekbones in the low lights and her insecurity drained away.

'You are more beautiful than anything I've ever seen before.'

Edie ducked her head. She was sure that she *wasn't*—at all—but she didn't want to let reality intrude right now. Insinctively she reached out and curled her hand around him.

He sucked in a breath as she tentatively moved her hand up and down, exploring the potency of his body, the glide of hot silky skin over steel. So vulnerable but so strong.

And then he put his hand over hers, stopping her. She looked up, feeling dazed. Drunk.

'Stop…or I'll lose it right here and now.'

A very feminine thrill moved through her at the glazed look in his eyes. To know that *she* was doing this to him… She'd wanted to see him lose control and it was headier than she'd imagined.

'Lie down, Edie.'

She did as he asked, realising that her legs were feeling seriously weak. Sebastio's gaze was tracking down over her body and emotion pricked her again. She ruthlessly pushed it down. This was no time for emotion. This was fantasy fulfilment, pure and simple. Karma. Ridding herself of the burden of innocence.

And it had been a burden, she realised now, even if she'd kept it to the back of her mind. Insidious doubt had been growing. What if something was wrong with her? What if something had been damaged during her cancer treatment? Her hormones? Her libido?

But the way she felt now allayed all those doubts and fears. She just hadn't met the right man. Or she had, but four years ago. And now…

Thankfully he came down on the bed beside her, and her thoughts were fast eclipsed by a surge of lust and need when he skated his hand tantalisingly down over her breasts, and then her belly, and down further to the juncture between her legs.

He applied a little pressure and she opened her legs. She saw intense concentration on his face. She realised she trusted him. Really trusted him.

She quickly pushed away that revelation.

His fingers were exploring now, between her legs, and her breath hitched when they parted the folds of flesh, releasing the damp heat that had been building there.

She could feel herself, slick against his fingers, and she

might have been embarrassed if he hadn't said, with a definite note of satisfaction in his voice, 'You're so ready...'

Edie tried not to squirm against him, her hands clutching the sheet underneath her body. Tension rose as his fingers thrust inside her and her back arched off the bed. She bit her lip, trying to lessen the intense pleasure as he moved them slowly in and out. Tension coiled tighter and tighter, until she was afraid she'd explode like she had the other night, exposing her inexperience. She held on with every atom of control she could muster...

Sebastio was so hard he hurt. He was torturing himself as much as Edie by prolonging the pleasure. He could see the mute pleading on her face, feel her body quiver around his hand... He needed to be inside her but he also needed to see her come. Now. Like this. At his mercy. On some level it was restoring a desperate need to feel some semblance of still being in control.

He felt the tremors in her legs, in her whole body, as she fought to hang on and he bent over and kissed her, saying, 'Let go... I'll catch you...' just as he thrust his fingers deep inside her, feeling her body lose its grip on control. She went wild, spasming with pleasure around his hand.

It almost pushed him over the edge of his own fraying control to feel how tight she was. He knew he wouldn't last much longer.

Sebastio moved over Edie's body, spreading her legs further apart. Her cheeks were pink and her eyes slightly unfocused in the aftermath of pleasure. Her mouth was swollen. He felt a surge of very masculine pride.

He smoothed some damp hair off her forehead. 'Okay?'

After a long moment she nodded. Her hands came up and circled his biceps. He moved between her legs, notching his erection against the exquisite damp heat of her body.

Four years of abstinence had not prepared Sebastio for this overload of anticipation…

He gritted his teeth and clung on to his control just for a little longer. He pushed into her body, feeling its resistance, and rested there for a moment, letting her get used to him. Even if it was killing him.

She brought her legs up around his waist and tilted her body up, making him slide in a little more. Sebastio was lost, drowning in an inferno of need. He needed this like he needed oxygen.

He said, 'This might hurt a little at first, but trust me it won't last…'

He gave in to the screaming dictates of his body and thrust deep, aware of Edie's wide eyes and sharp intake of breath.

He was embedded in the most pure sensation of pleasure he'd ever experienced. He needed to move…or die. He looked at her and something silent passed between them. They were beyond words.

She nodded her head, jerkily, and with as much control as he could muster Sebastio started to move in and out, his passage growing easier as he felt Edie's body adapt to his…

Edie was in meltdown as she tried to keep up with the maelstrom of feelings and sensations coursing through her. The stinging pain had been indescribable when Sebastio had thrust inside her at first, but it was fading now. He was big…big enough to make her breathless…but as her body got used to his suddenly it didn't feel that way any more.

She quickly became ravenous, seeking a deeper connection. She wrapped her legs around his waist even tighter, feeling the firm muscled globes of his buttocks under her heels.

Tension coiled to breaking point and the nirvana that

Edie had just experienced beckoned again. Except this time she knew it was going to be even better. More explosive.

She wrapped her arms around Sebastio's neck and arched her back, pressing her breasts against his chest. He curled an arm under her back, drawing her even closer, and when the pinnacle came it hit so hard and fast that all she could do was bite his shoulder to stop herself from screaming until she was hoarse.

The first thing Edie noticed when she woke was how heavy and replete she felt. Utterly exhausted and yet…energised. It was disconcerting. She opened her eyes and it took a moment of disorientation before the previous hours came rushing back in Technicolor.

The shutters on the windows were pushed back, and there were no curtains, like in the other rooms, so she could see that it was still dark outside.

She pulled the sheet up to her chest and looked around. She was alone, but she heard a noise from the bathroom. The door opened and Sebastio walked out with a towel around his waist, bare-chested. He must have been in the shower.

Instantly Edie felt awkward. She didn't know how to navigate this new post-coital world. This new cataclysmic world.

'You're awake.'

Edie tried to sit up, holding the sheet to herself. She looked around ineffectually for something to put on and Sebastio came into her line of vision, holding out a robe.

She took it. 'Thank you.'

'I've run you a bath—you'll be sore.'

Edie could feel it. The tenderness between her legs. But it wasn't sore. It felt…amazing. But Sebastio sounded cool. Solicitous. She was afraid to look at him as she dragged on the robe while trying not to expose herself. Ridiculous, considering that not long ago she'd been totally at his mercy, naked and utterly vulnerable.

She sat on the edge of the bed. 'I should go back to my own room. I can have a bath there.'

Except right now the thought of washing Sebastio's touch and scent off her body was anathema to Edie.

He said from above her, 'There's something we need to talk about.'

She looked up but she couldn't make out his expression in the dim lighting. A shiver of trepidation went down her spine. 'What?'

She saw his jaw clench. 'We didn't use protection.'

It took a second for the meaning of this to sink in, and as it did Edie's hand instinctively came up to touch the scar under her collarbone. She stopped herself from touching it at the last moment.

She forced words out through a dry mouth. 'It's fine. You don't need to worry about that.'

He frowned. 'Are you on the pill?'

She shook her head. 'No. But I had some…medical issues when I was a teenager and I can't get pregnant.'

Her periods were still completely irregular, even four years on, and the doctor had told her that it was highly unlikely she would conceive because of the treatment she'd undergone. Certainly she didn't expect her minute chance of getting pregnant to have occurred in this situation. It was unlikely enough to be impossible.

'Are you sure?' He sounded sceptical.

Edie nodded and stood up, belting the robe around her. She could see the detritus of her clothes spread around the room and cringed inwardly, remembering how she'd all but stormed into Sebastio's study and demanded he sleep with her.

Sebastio studied Edie. To his surprise he found that he believed she was telling the truth about not getting pregnant. He wondered what had affected her fertility, but then he saw her biting her lip and put out a hand, tugging it free. Even that small movement made his recently sated body come back to roaring life.

She said, 'I… I should go back to my room.'

He shook his head, battling an irrational urge to lock his door and never let her out of his sight. One thing was certain after that conflagration: once would not be enough with this woman. Not by a long shot.

'There's no need for that… Have your bath and then we'll get some food. I have no intention of letting you rest for too long.'

She looked at him, her eyes growing wide as she understood his meaning. Quickly followed by a faint blush.

Sebastio groaned. 'Edie…bath. *Now*. Unless you want to test your energy reserves before we eat?'

# CHAPTER SIX

EDIE LOOKED ACROSS at Sebastio where he sat at the end of the dining table. He'd insisted on bringing food up here from the kitchen and she felt like giggling when she thought of how they must look, eating omelettes and bread and drinking wine in a room that was more used to high-society gatherings.

After her bath Sebastio had dressed Edie in a pair of his sweats, tying the waist tight, and one of his sweatshirts. It drowned her, but she guiltily relished his scent around her. He'd put on jeans and a loose shirt.

He sat back now. 'What?'

Edie shrugged, feeling embarrassed to have been caught staring. She said the first thing she could think of. 'Your bedroom—it's not done up like the other rooms… Why is it so bare?'

He shrugged. 'When I gave instructions to redecorate the lodge I told the interior designers they had carte blanche in every room except my bedroom. I have no interest in how the house is done up. I mainly use it for corporate events. I prefer to keep things simple. My penthouse is modern, clean—it reflects more of my personal taste.' He waved a hand to indicate the plush luxurious furnishings in the rest of the house. 'This place, these furnishings, it's what people expect to see.'

'Just like the Christmas decorations, even though you hate Christmas?'

He took a sip of wine and she saw the gleam in his eye—a warning not to stray too far down this path. 'Exactly.'

Through the window behind Sebastio Edie could see dawn stealing across the sky. The entire world was white and still, and as she took another sip of wine she'd never felt more decadent. Or more alive.

Sebastio put his wine glass down and stood up, holding out his hand. She took it, letting him pull her up. Without words he led her back up the stairs to the bedroom.

Edie knew what this was—a very finite and fleeting moment of madness while they were in this bubble. She had to keep reminding herself of that, no matter what happened.

When Edie woke again it was dark outside. Shock hit her when she realised that a whole day had passed.

She suspected that if the world hadn't ground to a halt as spectacularly as it had outside Sebastio wouldn't have been so keen to let the days and nights melt into one another, blurring the passage of time. She had the sense that ordinarily the boundary lines with his lovers would be very well marked.

And she didn't think it was because she was different—no matter what her tripping pulse might tell her. It was because they'd been forced into this abnormal situation by forces outside their control.

Sebastio had turned on the TV earlier, and they'd watched news of massive blizzards and treacherous conditions across Britain. There was a national alert for people to stay indoors unless absolutely necessary.

Edie had had a text from her parents, asking if she was okay, and she'd blushed as she'd responded. They thought she was tucked up in her flat.

She turned her head now and looked at Sebastio, lying beside her. Her breath hitched. He was so beautiful. The covers rode down low, barely covering his sex. She could see the start of the dark hair curling between his legs and it was incredibly erotic.

She was amazed that he retained that slightly guarded look even in his sleep, and had to stop herself from reaching out to smooth the line in his brow.

What he had done to her…what they had done together… Her mind was still shying away from looking at it too closely. Like not looking directly at the sun. The pleasure he'd wrung from her body with such ruthless precision… It overwhelmed her even now just to think of it.

For a long time, when she'd been ill, she'd never thought she'd feel comfortable or at ease in her skin again. Sebastio had returned something very precious to her: her confidence in herself as a sexual woman. She wasn't cold, or frigid. She hadn't been irrevocably damaged…

Her heart squeezed. Apart from her fertility. Which was not something a man like Sebastio ever needed to care about. She would be long gone from his life before anything like that would need to be discussed.

At that moment Sebastio made a low groaning sound. Edie tensed. She realised that there was a faint sheen of persipiration on his skin. The frown lines on his face seemed deeper.

Then he jerked upright in the bed with such a sudden movement that Edie sat up too, her heart pounding. He cried out in Spanish, in a hoarse voice, a stream of words that Edie couldn't understand.

All she could make out was *'Por Dios!'* and *'No!'*

He was gasping now, caught in the grip of whatever nightmare was in his head. Edie tentatively reached out a hand and touched him on the shoulder. His skin was burning up.

Suddenly he went very still, his breathing laboured. Edie could see his focus coming into the room. She wasn't sure if she should have touched him, but he'd sounded so anguished...

'Sebastio...? You were having a dream.'

Sebastio was still somewhere halfway between that horrific night and the present moment...holding Maya's lifeless body in his hands while hearing Victor scream in pain from the car...and there had been nothing he could do.

Slowly it receded and the room came into focus. And something else. Edie's voice. Cool and calm. Her hand on his shoulder.

It was too much. He couldn't bear to look at her and see the way her eyes would fill with something he couldn't accept. How could he ever accept anything but condemnation?

He jerked away from her hand and pushed back the covers, getting out of bed. His legs were pathetically weak. He said curtly, 'Go back to your own bed, Edie. I'm sorry I disturbed you.'

He couldn't even look at her. He went straight into his bathroom and closed the door. He stood in the dark for a long moment, letting his heart come back to normal... He hadn't had that dream for a long time. And he'd never had it in the presence of a lover.

Edie... It wasn't her fault he'd had the dream. *Nightmare.* But she'd got under his skin to a raw part of him where too many wounds lay in wait. He could still feel the touch of her small cool hand on his shoulder. Like a balm. A balm he didn't want or need.

He cursed and ignored the urge to go and check to see if she'd gone back to her own room. He flicked a light on and looked at his reflection in the mirror. His messy hair and stubbled jaw. Eyes still wild after the dream.

Any measure of peace he might have felt over the past thirty-six hours had been just an illusion. A by-product of sating his lust for the first time in four years.

And Edie wasn't solely responsible for that, he told himself with not a little sense of desperation. Any woman would have made him feel the same way. It was purely biological.

The awful tentacles of the nightmare still clung to him like a grey mist, mocking him.

He cursed and went into the shower, flicking it on. The water pummelled his body, but not even that could dispel the lingering horror...

Edie sat on the bed, torn even though Sebastio had told her to leave. He'd looked...tortured. She heard the shower. She got up, intending to leave and give Sebastio his space, but then from inside the bathroom she heard the sound of a guttural cry.

A shiver went through her. It sounded animalistic. Pure pain.

Knowing he might not thank her for it, but unable to leave, Edie tentatively opened the bathroom door. She saw Sebastio in the huge walk-in shower. His back was to her and his hands were on the wall. Water ran down the planes and muscles of his back and buttocks. There was no steam. He had to be standing under a cold shower.

*No.* Her heart squeezed. She went in and dropped her robe to the ground. She went over to the shower and it was freezing. She reached for the control and turned the water to warm.

Sebastio looked around, and the pain etched on his face nearly felled her.

He said roughly, 'I told you to leave, Edie.'

'I'm not going anywhere.'

The water was warm now, steam starting to rise. Edie stepped behind Sebastio and put her arms around his waist, resting her cheek against his back. She could feel the tension in his body, the rigid rejection of compassion or comfort. But she just held on tighter. Water was plastering her hair to her skull, running down into her eyes. But she didn't care.

He brought his hands to hers and she thought he was going to pull them apart. But after a long moment he covered them with his and a shudder racked his body. And then another.

After long moments of just standing like that Sebastio switched them round, so that Edie was standing against the wall and he was in front of her. He put one arm on the wall behind her head and his other one on her hip.

The pain on his face had turned into something else. Something more primal. His eyes burned and a whole new tension came into the space between them. A tension she recognised and that made her nerve-endings sizzle.

'I need you, Edie. Now…here. But I don't think I can be gentle… If you want to go, go now…'

Edie understood in an instant. It resonated inside her. He needed to expel whatever darkness held him in its grip. He needed *her*. Her heart expanded in her chest before she could stop it. She knew the wise thing to do would be to walk away, but she could no more do that than stop breathing.

She put her hands on Sebastio's chest and felt his heartbeat thundering. 'Take me. I'm yours.'

He looked as if he was wrestling with himself inwardly for a moment, and Edie reached down and took his erection in her hand, slowly stroking him. His eyes became glazed, his breathing laboured.

And then all bets were off. Edie had flung herself into the eye of the storm and all she could do was hang on.

Sebastio was remorseless. He came down on his knees, pushed her legs apart and buried his face between her legs, sucking and licking at her very core until she was begging for mercy and her legs were shaking.

In the shattering aftermath of her orgasm Sebastio lifted her against the wall and instructed her roughly, 'Put your legs around my waist.'

Her breath caught as he positioned himself and drove up into her body with such precision and strength that she could only wrap her arms and legs tight around him and rush headlong with him, wherever he was taking her.

It was brutal, the pleasure he wrung from her body before taking his own. That was the only way Edie could describe it. Brutally exquisite. All-encompassing. Shattering.

She was barely aware of him holding her there. His body jerking spasmodically against hers. The warm rush of his release inside her.

Eventually he let her down, but her legs wouldn't take her weight and so he wrapped her in a towel and carried her to the bed. She had a vague memory of Sebastio whispering something before she fell into a deep dreamless sleep, and she thought it might have been *thank you*.

When Edie woke again bright sunlight was streaming in through the bedroom window. The events of the previous night came rushing back. She remembered Sebastio telling her to leave. And then how he'd shuddered in her arms in the shower. The desperation on his face. The scorching hot combustion. And then…oblivion.

She was naked under the covers and she blushed, thinking of what had happened, how intense it had been. How…*raw*.

And again later, when they'd both woken ravenous for each other. It was as if an immense hunger had been uncovered and would never be sated...

The bed beside her was empty, and Edie looked around the room. In the stark daylight she realised just how bare his bedroom really was. He'd told her his style was pared back. Simple. But this was like a monk's cell—in total contrast to the rest of the house.

She wondered if there was something more to it than just his style preference. Somehow it felt almost...punishing. Like the way he'd been standing under that cold shower last night.

There was no sound from the bathroom. She was alone. A tiny cold dart scored her heart as she had to acknowledge the fact that Sebastio might have sought comfort from her but he wouldn't welcome admitting it.

And what had she expected? That he'd be lying here, watching her sleep, waiting for her to wake? That he would want to tell her all the gory details of why he'd had a nightmare? She was no stranger to those—she'd had them for years during her treatment, and she'd certainly never wanted to articulate them to anyone.

She got up and found the sweatpants she'd been wearing before, and the loose shirt that Sebastio had been wearing, pulling them on haphazardly. His scent was on her skin. The scent of *them*. She didn't want to wash it off.

She left the room in search of Sebastio, feeling a little nervous at the thought of seeing him again after last night. But she couldn't dampen the flutter in her belly. The very illicit feeling that they'd shared something the previous night. Something profound.

She finally heard his voice through his study door, deep and authoritative. At the last moment she didn't knock and go in—she turned and went down to the kitchens.

A half hour later she was climbing back up to the main hall with a tray holding two plates of warm pancakes, maple syrup, crispy bacon and a steaming pot of coffee. Along with two glasses of freshly squeezed orange juice.

She couldn't stop the goofy smile on her face at the thought of surprising him with breakfast, and was almost across the hall before she noticed that the front door was open and Matteo was stepping inside, stamping his feet and shaking off some snow.

He smiled at Edie. '*Buon giorno!* You survived!'

Edie blinked. The sight of another person was so incongruous that it took her a long moment to realise what was happening. She could hear vehicles outside. Voices. She could see patches of green. The snow was thawing. Had thawed.

For a moment she felt totally disorientated, and then there was another voice. Far more familiar.

Sebastio had come out of his office and was greeting Matteo. Edie realised she was standing in the middle of the grand hall in her bare feet. No make-up. She was wearing Sebastio's clothes. She was holding a tray of food for lovers. She'd even plucked some ivy leaves from one of her displays and put them in a small vase.

And now Sebastio was turning to look at her, his eyes widening as he took in what she was holding. The way she was dressed. In contrast to Edie he was pristine. Dressed in a suit. Had he known the real world was about to rush back in? Stupidly she felt betrayed.

Before she could mortify herself any more she turned and fled back the way she'd come, almost tripping down the stairs to the kitchen in her haste. She had visions of staff arriving and tipped the food from the plates into a bin, before washing up and getting rid of the evidence of her stupidly misplaced hope...

*For what?* she castigated herself. Hope that these past couple of days and nights had meant something to Sebastio? When he'd expressly told her that he wasn't interested in anything?

She heard a noise behind her and tensed.

'Edie?'

She closed her eyes for a moment and sucked in a fortifying breath before turning around and praying for a convincing show of nonchalance. Sebastio was looking at her, and she rushed to fill the silence before he could say anything.

'I'm sorry. I should have realised that—'

'Edie, you don't have to explain—'

'I didn't know the snow had melted.'

Sebastio's chest felt tight. The expression of horror on Edie's face in the hall was etched into his memory. Clearly she'd had no idea that normal service was about to resume. That she'd slept until almost lunchtime.

He hadn't gone to disturb her because, selfishly, a perverse part of him had relished the thought of her still sleeping in his bed, naked.

When he'd seen her in the hall, wearing his clothes, barefoot and looking so deliciously rumpled, his brain had short-circuited. And then he'd realised that Matteo was also looking at her and that she was carrying a tray of food. For them.

He'd been as guilty as her of assuming—*hoping?*—the world hadn't started to turn again. He'd only realised that the thaw had set in at exactly the same moment his phone had started ringing off the hook.

After stealing out of the bedroom and dealing with some calls he'd gone back upstairs and washed and changed, and as he'd looked at Edie sleeping in his bed, he'd selfisly left her there, her image burned onto his retina.

He'd wanted to take her back to her own room last night

after the shower, but at the last moment he'd given in to a weak urge and let her sleep in his bed. He'd sat in a chair in the corner of the room and looked at her for a long time. Watching the soft rise and fall of her chest.

He should have felt angry at his lapse of control, for letting her see so much. But all he had felt was a curious kind of… He didn't want to say *peace*. Maybe calm. A moment of catharsis.

And now it mocked him, because of the way he'd allowed the lines to become blurred thanks to a bit of snow and an over-indulgence of pleasure. He should have been more vigilant.

Now Edie had no expression on her face and that frustrated him. 'I'm sorry. I should have warned you that everyone was coming back… I didn't think you'd—'

She put up a hand. 'Please, don't say anything. I should have noticed myself…'

*If I'd looked out of the window instead of superstitiously hoping nothing would change if I didn't,* Edie thought.

Sebastio ran a hand through his hair. Edie couldn't fail once again to notice how put-together he was compared to her. In control. Not affected.

'Look, what we had for the past few days…and nights… it was intense. But I should have been more careful to make it clear that this is just—'

'Sebastio, stop…' Edie cut in, horrified that he felt the need to reiterate what he'd told her before. 'You don't need to say anything. I know that it was…intense. Maybe not what either of us were expecting… But you don't need to worry. I'm not falling for you or anything like that.'

*Liar.*

She could feel heat rising and she rushed on. 'I will admit that four years ago…when I approached you and you rejected me… I might have harboured a fantasy that things had turned out differently. Well, now they have…and that's all this is for me. The fulfilment of a fantasy.'

Edie held her breath. She was beyond mortified at having to spell out the fact that she'd thought about him for four years. But better that than his obvious suspicion that she was falling for him in spite of his warning.

And she wasn't, she told herself fiercely. She couldn't be. She was smarter than that.

Sebastio felt a mix of emotions. None of which he should be feeling. Edie looked so earnest he couldn't *not* believe her. She clearly hated admitting it. And yet it wasn't relief he was feeling to know that he'd simply fulfilled a fantasy. It was something closer to disgruntlement.

He hated to admit it, but to think he was just some kind of box she'd ticked was seriously irritating. And he didn't like the thought that he would merely be the first in a long line of lovers.

Voices came from above. Staff returning.

Edie looked panicked. 'I should go and get dressed. There's a lot of work to do before the party tomorrow night.'

Sebastio stood back to let her pass. 'Of course.'

Their scent reached his nostrils. The scent of them together. It was unbelievably erotic and had an immediate effect on Sebastio's arousal levels, which were constantly raised when this woman was near. As much as he wished he had burned through his desire for her over the space of a weekend, clearly it wasn't going to be that simple.

He caught her arm as she was about to walk past him. He felt the tension in her body. She looked at him. Eyes huge. Dark blue.

'This isn't over, Edie.'

She didn't say anything. Just pulled her arm free and went upstairs.

Sebastio curbed the urge to go after her and remind her

ABBY GREEN                                      117

of what they'd shared over the past couple of days. He had the uncomfortable feeling that something had just slipped out of his grasp.

The following evening Edie was no less confused about Sebastio's declaration. *'This isn't over.'*

She paced back and forth in her bedroom, eyeing the glossy black box on her bed. Another box. Containing another beautiful dress to seduce her with?

Edie knew she wanted Sebastio. He didn't need to buy her beautiful dresses in order to seduce her. She couldn't imagine a day when she wouldn't want him. That was what scared her.

When she had seen the helicopter arriving and taking off yesterday she'd felt relieved for a second, thinking that Sebastio's absence might actually help her rationalise how she was feeling. And then Matteo had given her a note.

> *I have to go into town. I'll be back tomorrow in time*
> *for the party.*
> *I want you there, Edie.*
> SR

Suddenly she'd been in turmoil again. She'd felt excitement, desire and panic, all mixed together. Panic because she really wasn't sure she could let this go any further without getting seriously hurt.

She stopped and looked at the box as if it was a ticking bomb. Eventually, because she couldn't resist, she went and opened it, pushing back the layers of gold tissue paper. *Gold!*

She lifted out a dress so stunning in its elegant simplicity that she gasped. It was black lace with a nude lining. Off the shoulder, long and straight. Cap sleeves. The material was so delicate it felt like air in her hands.

There were matching black shoes and underwear. A strapless bra. Panties. Stockings.

It was bad enough that she'd actually told Sebastio she'd fantasised about being with him. It was as if there was no corner of her mind that he wasn't privy to now. And Edie knew that if she was to indulge in this for a moment longer she'd be heading for a fall she might never recover from.

She was nothing to Sebastio. An anomaly. A fleeting moment of lust that would soon burn out for him.

She put the dress back in the box. She couldn't do this. She'd never been someone who couldn't face up to reality and now she *really* needed to face up to reality.

# CHAPTER SEVEN

'SHE'S WHAT?'

'She's gone, Sebastio. She left with Jimmy earlier. There's a note in your office.'

For a moment after Matteo had walked away, Sebastio simply did not believe what he'd said. No one walked away from him. Not since he'd been a child, when he'd become so inured to watching his parents walk away that he'd vowed never to let anyone else have that power over him.

He felt as if someone had just punched him in the chest. Winded. That sensation he'd had the previous day of something slipping out of his grasp mocked him.

He went into his office and closed the door behind him. He saw the small piece of paper on his desk and went over. Something else was starting to fill him now. Anger.

He picked it up. Read the neat, concise writing.

*Dear Sebastio,*
*I hope you won't be too inconvenienced if I leave now, as the last party is tonight.*
*    I hope you'll find that everything is in order. I will, of course, be back to ensure the efficient removal of the Christmas dressing at an appropriate time.*

*Thank you for the opportunities you've given me,*
*Sebastio.*
*All the best,*
*Edie*

He stared at it for a long minute.

*Thank you for the opportunities...*

Was she including the unburdening of her innocence
in that? Sebastio had a white-hot memory flash of how it
had felt to thrust into Edie's body that first time. The exquisite torture of it as he'd had to control himself so as not
to hurt her.

His first cynical thought was that she was playing some
game. Running away so he'd go after her. But almost immediately it rang hollow. She didn't play games. She wouldn't
know how.

Sebastio threw the note down and went to the window
of his office. He could see the guests arriving now in their
droves and he felt sick.

The black and white of his tuxedo was reflected in the
window. He'd never felt like this before—unmoored.

Why the hell had she left?

It was Christmas Eve and Edie was walking home from
the local shop, where everyone had been panic-buying before everything shut down in a few hours. The beautiful,
pristine snow had turned to slush in the last few days and
the air was bitingly cold with thick leaden skies overhead.

The glinting, winking Christmas lights and decorations
nearby looked garish and cheap, and Edie told herself a little caustically that Sebastio had ruined her for Christmas.

She tried not to think of Sebastio and what his reaction

would have been when he got her note. He wouldn't have been happy, because he didn't like anything happening that wasn't on his terms. But she figured that he wouldn't have been too bothered. He would have gone down to the party and soon forgotten about Edie.

She clamped down on the stupid sense of self-pity. She'd never indulged in it before and wasn't about to start now.

She'd spoken to her parents earlier, and they'd sounded so delighted with themselves in the Bahamas that it had made up for everything.

*Even falling for Sebastio?* a small voice whispered.

Edie fiercely denied it to herself, but it rang hollow.

Jimmy had been sweet enough to invite Edie to spend Christmas Day with him and his family, but she'd declined, preferring the thought of being alone so she could try and get over the impact Sebastio had had on her life.

*On her heart.*

As she approached the tall white house where she lived on the top floor, she told herself stoutly that lots of people spent Christmas alone. With no decorations. Or presents. Or a fancy turkey dinner with all the trimmings. She could do this. She'd be fine.

But her treacherous mind automatically wandered to what Sebastio would be doing for Christmas. Maybe he'd already left the country now that his social engagements were over?

So when Edie heard her name being called by a familiar voice she thought she was having an aural hallucination. She scowled as she stuck her key in the door, but it came again, with a trace of irritation this time.

'*Edie...*'

The irritation convinced her it must be real. She turned around slowly, to see Sebastio standing at the bottom of the steps leading up to her house. She blinked. He didn't disappear.

He was dressed in black trousers and a black top. A long dark overcoat with the collar turned up. When she allowed herself to believe he wasn't an apparition giddy joy rushed through her before she could stop it. She'd really believed she wouldn't see him again.

And then the joy was diluted by a delayed sense of self-preservation kicking in. She came down until she was at his eye level on the bottom step. Somehow it didn't make her feel as if she had any advantage.

'Sebastio. What are you doing here?'

He looked grim. 'Why did you leave before the party?'

Edie glanced away for a moment. And then back. She moved aside to let some people up the steps. She saw their curious glances at Sebastio, and then he caught her arm and tugged her aside. Even through her thick Puffa jacket she could feel the impact of his touch, her nerve-endings tingling.

'Edie, we can't talk here. Let's go up to your apartment.'

Panic spiked at the thought of being alone with him in her tiny intimate space. 'No.'

'Please.'

She looked at him. His mouth was tense.

'I'm not leaving till you agree to talk to me. We can do it here, or at my apartment in Mayfair.'

Edie knew very well she was no match for Sebastio's determination. Something gave way inside her. 'Okay, your apartment. But I'm not staying for long.'

He inclined his head. 'Of course. You can leave whenever you wish.'

He stood back and a driver jumped out of the vehicle behind Sebastio to open the door. Edie took a breath and stepped forward, getting in with her shopping bags. Sebastio got in on the other side, immediately dwarfing the space. His scent wound around Edie like a siren call. A male siren call.

The vehicle pulled into the street and Edie absorbed the shock still reverberating through her body.

Sebastio asked, 'You were shopping?'

She looked at the plastic bags she was still clutching like shields and put them down at her feet. 'Just some supplies for the next couple of days, when the shops are shut.' The kind of thing a man like Sebastio wouldn't have to worry about with the world at his beck and call 24/7.

'You're not going home for Christmas?'

She shook her head. 'My parents are away. I bought them a Caribbean cruise as a gift for Christmas.'

'With the money I paid you?'

Edie looked at Sebastio. 'Does it matter?'

'No… You can do what you want with the money. So,' he continued, 'you are going to be spending Christmas alone?'

'Yes.'

There was a long moment of silence before Sebastio said, 'You could spend Christmas with me.'

Edie looked at him as something helpless flowed through her. A sense of inevitability. 'Sebastio…*no*.'

Sebastio merely pushed a button in the partition between the front and the back of the car and the privacy window slid up with a slight hiss. The tinted windows lent the back of the car a cocoon-like aspect.

He moved closer and Edie was rooted to the seat. She could see the dark flecks of grey in his eyes. The line of stubble on his jaw. The thick luxuriousness of his hair.

He had taken her woollen cap off her head before she could stop him, and he threw it somewhere behind him.

'Hey…' she said, but it sounded weak. Ineffectual.

*Spend Christmas with me.*

He was bending towards her, giving her time to pull

back. To say no. But she couldn't form the words. All she could see was his mouth, and she felt so hungry to taste him again. He stopped a few inches away. Torturously. Testing her will. And Edie knew then that she didn't have the strength to deny this man. No matter what the cost.

She reached out and put her hands on his coat, pulled him forward. Their mouths crashed together and Sebastio reached all the way around her to pull her to his body. She was ravenous for him. Desperate.

After long minutes of re-tasting and relearning, Sebastio pulled back. Edie was barely aware that the car was moving and London was passing by outside. They could have been on the moon.

He shook his head. 'Why would you deny yourself this?'

At that precise moment Edie was wondering exactly the same thing. *This* was vital to her well-being. A life-force coursing through her veins and arteries. Right now she thought she'd die without it. Even if it would kill her in the end—emotionally.

Edie wasn't unaware of the irony. She knew that falling for Sebastio and continuing the affair when she knew it was bad for her wasn't a million miles away from taking chemotherapy—which had been as toxic as it had been beneficial.

A little giggle escaped her as a kind of euphoric hysteria gripped her for a minute. Then she stopped and reached up to touch his jaw, tracing the hard line.

'Yes,' she whispered. 'I'll spend Christmas with you.'

Sebastio felt intense satisfaction and not a little triumph. Things he wouldn't usually associate with women. When he'd seen Edie on the street, walking back to her drab-looking house on a very pedestrian street, he'd had to battle the compulsion to open the door, grab her, pull her into the car and take her far away. He'd had to force himself to be civilised.

He had her now. That was all that mattered.

He smiled, feeling a sense of lightness pervade him. He almost didn't recognise what it was. Then he took out his phone and made a call to his assistant, issuing a curt instruction to 'Go ahead with the plan as soon as possible.'

'What plan?' Edie asked when he'd terminated the call.

'You'll see,' he said enigmatically, before setting about removing her coat so that he could put his hands on her slender curves with nothing in the way.

By the time they reached Sebastio's Mayfair apartment dusk was falling. Edie struggled to sit up from where she'd fallen asleep, all but draped across Sebastio's chest. She remembered he'd been kissing her to the point of dizziness before his phone had rung and he'd reluctantly stopped, saying he needed to take the call. He'd sat up straight, clamping her to his side, and his deep sonorous tones speaking in Spanish had lulled her into sleep.

She realised now with a little jolt how *safe* she'd felt. Truly safe—as if nothing could harm her. But she knew all too well how much danger there was, and that it wasn't always something she could be protected from. Not even by a man as seemingly invincible as Sebastio Rivas.

He got out of the car now and bent down, extending his hand to Edie. 'Come on.'

She hesitated for a second, her sense of self-preservation kicking in very belatedly. But then she pictured herself refusing to go with Sebastio. Taking the Tube back home. Going into her small, bare apartment. Curling up and feeling cold…

His hand was so close. His sheer vitality reached out to her. *She wanted him.* She couldn't walk away.

She put her hand into his and let him lead her up to his penthouse apartment.

* * *

Edie had never been in a top-floor apartment before. She'd rarely ever been at the top of any high building—unless she counted a school trip to the London Eye when she was fourteen.

But as she walked in behind Sebastio, holding her coat over her arm, the breath left her body. It was beyond spectacular. Every wall seemed to be made of glass, giving a 360-degree view of London.

The furnishings were modern and low-key, with abstract art dotted around the space. The dark grey colour scheme and dark wood furniture was unmistakably masculine.

She walked over to one of the main windows. The rooftops of Mayfair were spread out on one side, and Buckingham Palace looked close enough to touch. She could see the London Eye, and she was pretty sure they were higher. The Thames snaked through London. St Paul's dome pierced the sky in the far distance.

Sebastio stood beside her. She felt more than a little overwhelmed, and tried to say as lightly as she could, 'You know how to pick your properties.'

She felt him shrug. 'It was the best on offer at the time.'

She dragged her gaze off the view to look at him. 'You really couldn't care less, could you?'

There was a flicker of something so fleeting across his face that she almost missed it. It had looked like pain. 'No. Surroundings don't interest me too much.'

She knew he meant it. He would be as dominant and as at home in a ground-floor duplex. But he would be expected to be in a place like this. Just as people would expect to see his house beautifully dressed for Christmas in Richmond.

She thought of his sparsely furnished bedroom in the lodge and how it had felt like some sort of punishment. Like when he'd been under cold water in the shower. She felt intuitively that this behaviour was a direct result from the crash, almost as if he'd put his life on hold. Not allowing himself to live.

Interrupting her thoughts, he asked, 'Why did you leave before the party?'

She looked away again. A million and one things flitted through her head, but in the end she could only be brutally honest. 'Because I wanted to stay too much. Your world is very seductive. But it's not my world. I thought it would be better to make a clean break. I didn't think you'd notice.'

Edie would prefer for him to think his world had been more seductive to her than him.

He put his hands on her shoulders and turned her around. 'Well, I did notice. Very much.'

Edie thought of the dress and felt a pang of regret. 'I know this isn't going to last, Sebastio—'

He put a finger on her mouth, stopping her. 'Do you still want me?'

She fought not to roll her eyes at how obvious that answer must be. She just nodded.

He dropped his finger. 'I still want you too. Let's just spend a little more time together and see what happens.'

Edie's heart-rate increased. *See what happens...*

Then he said, 'I have plans for this evening...'

Edie felt a rush of disappointment so acute that she almost didn't hear him go on.

'You have half an hour to get ready and we're going out.'

She looked at him, relief filling her that he'd meant for those plans to include her. 'Out? But nothing will be open— it's Christmas Eve.'

His mouth tipped up slightly. 'It's London.'

She indicated her worn jeans and shapeless top. 'I didn't exactly come prepared.'

'Don't worry about that. I'll show you your room.'

Bemused, Edie followed him down a long corridor to where he opened a door to the bedroom. It was elegantly understated, with a huge bed and sleek modern furniture with an art deco twist. The floor-to-ceiling windows showcased another breathtaking view.

'My room is through the adjoining door. Obviously we'll be sharing a bed, Edie… But this is your space.'

She looked at him and longed to make some kind of smart remark, to dent that arrogance even a little. But of course she was going to share his bed. That was the only reason she was here, wasn't it?

He opened another door, artfully hidden in the wall panel, to reveal a dressing room and an en-suite bathroom. She walked in to see clothes hanging from hangers and shelves full of folded clothes.

She picked up a pair of jeans. Her size exactly. She gasped and looked at Sebastio. 'These are for me?'

He nodded and came forward and plucked something from behind her, holding it up. It was the stunning black lace dress. Edie's breath stopped.

'Wear this tonight. Please.'

Edie took it from him. She really did feel like Alice in Wonderland now. Slipping down a rabbit hole she might never find her way out of again.

'Okay…'

He backed out of the room. 'Half an hour, Edie.'

Half an hour later Sebastio was looking out of the same window Edie had gravitated towards when she'd first walked in, her eyes popping out of her head. He was ashamed to admit it, but it had taken witnessing her reaction to remind him that not everyone felt a piercing stab of guilt when they recognised how lucky they were. Lucky to have these views. Lucky to have this stunning apartment and many more across the world. Lucky to be walking on both his legs.

*Lucky to be alive.*

At that moment he wondered if he'd done the right thing in bringing Edie here. Following the dictates of his ravenous hunger for her. She saw too much. She had seen too much. He could still recall how it had felt to have her arms sliding around him in that shower. The way she'd held on to him so tightly. The emotion that he'd been unable to hold back. The need to eclipse it with something else.

*Passion.*

He'd taken her like a caveman, up against the wall. And she'd let him. Her body had milked his for what had felt like aeons as he'd spent himself to the point of oblivion. An oblivion he'd never experienced before.

He heard a sound and turned around from the window. Any vague regret about bringing Edie here melted in a wave of heat and lust. She stood in the doorway and she looked like a goddess.

The dress moulded to her form, and for a second Sebastio thought she was naked underneath because all he could see was flesh. But then he realised it was a slip. Her shoulders were slender and straight. Her short cap of glossy hair highlighted the elegance of her long neck. She was spun from a fantasy Sebastio had never even known he'd had.

'You look…stunning.'

She walked into the room, endearingly unsure. Once again, fleetingly, Sebastio thought that if she was acting then she should be on the stage. For the first time he hated it that he was so cynical.

She stopped in front of him. 'Thank you. It's a beautiful dress. You shouldn't have.'

Sebastio desisted from telling her how much he was

looking forward to taking it off later. He just said, 'My driver is waiting—let's go.'

In the car, she asked, 'Where are we going?'

Sebastio brought her hand up to his mouth and kissed the back of it. 'Wait and see.'

He was surprised at how much he was enjoying teasing her, how much he was enjoying her reaction to everything. She was like an excited child. Eyes shining. If he wasn't very careful he might find her naive reactions more addictive than he'd like to admit.

Edie still didn't know where to look, even though they'd been there a couple of hours, lingering over dinner—tiny portions of food that looked more like art installations but which tasted sinfully rich and delicious.

The restaurant was luxurious and discreet. Tastefully lit and decorated for the festive season without being overpowering. Booths and artfully placed tables shielded guests from sight while not obscuring the eye-watering views. She and Sebastio shared one such booth, and as a waiter topped up their glasses of champagne he asked if they'd like any coffee.

Edie shook her head, not wanting to dilute the delicious feeling of slight disembodiment. It was like a dream she didn't want to wake up from. All she could see was London, laid out like a glittering shimmering carpet of Christmas lights. Magical.

And Sebastio.

She wasn't sure which view was more breathtaking, if she was honest. She could feel his eyes on her and it was heady and intoxicating. Like the way he'd made her feel when she'd seen his eyes widen on her earlier.

She felt beautiful under his gaze. When for so long she'd felt as if her body was somehow defective. It had been in arrested development for so long. She still didn't have regular periods...

'What's that mark...just under your collarbone?'

Immediately Edie went cold. Sebastio was looking at the scar from her port, where she'd received her chemo treatment. She raised her hand towards it instinctively. She'd not even noticed that it was visible because the neck of the dress was so low.

She swallowed. 'It's just a scar from an old injury.'

She took a sip of champagne, desperately wanting to change the subject.

Without really thinking, she asked, 'You must miss rugby a lot, if it was such a huge part of your life?'

She held her breath, immediately regretting asking him about that. But to her surprise his expression softened.

'I do miss it. More than anyone can understand...except maybe another retired player.'

Intrigued now, Edie asked, 'How did you get into it? It doesn't sound like a natural progression for someone due to inherit a banking business.'

He looked at her and said wryly, 'It wasn't. Far from it. But one summer I was sent to a camp outside Buenos Aires—after some transgression that had annoyed my father—and they had a rugby team. I played and realised I had a talent for it. I got hooked. The fact that it irritated the hell out of both my parents when I wanted to keep it up only made me more determined to do it. Then going to school in Europe helped to keep up my interest, as it's such a huge game there.'

'My father is a massive fan,' Edie said, feeling ridiculously shy. 'I think he was even at that match when you played in Edinburgh four years ago.'

'But you weren't?'

Edie shook her head, avoiding his eye. Somehow, they'd

circled back to the place she'd tried to steer him away from. 'I had other things on my mind…'

He took her hand, lacing his fingers with hers. 'Ready to go?'

Edie nodded, relieved that he was letting that one go. She'd been ready since he'd looked at her earlier. Her skin felt stretched tight over her bones. Awareness sizzled along her veins. Little fires danced wherever his eyes rested. Chasing away memories she didn't want to think about.

When they returned to the apartment Sebastio stopped in the doorway after opening the door. He pulled her around in front of him and put his hands over her eyes.

She brought her hands up over his. 'Sebastio… What…?'

But he was walking her into the apartment and she couldn't see a thing, so she just went with it. She felt tension come into his form when they stopped. She couldn't hear a sound.

'Sebastio…?'

He slowly drew his hands away and Edie's eyes took a second to adjust. When they did, and she took in the scene, she gasped. There was a massive Christmas tree in the corner, dressed with ornate ornaments and small candles that looked uncannily real but which she knew were ingenious LED lights.

Boxes of differing sizes were placed at the bottom of the tree, wrapped in silver and pink paper. And there were other decorations dotted around the sleek space, very tasteful and in keeping with the surroundings. There was an enticing smell of spices. Soft jazz was playing… Christmas classics.

She was stunned and not a little overwhelmed. Sebastio had done this for her? She was afraid to look at him in case he saw the emotion she was feeling.

'Do you like it?' He sounded uncharacterisically unsure.

She whispered, 'I love it… But I thought this was my job.'

He came in front of her, shaking his head. 'Your job with me is officially completed. I hired the company who worked under you at the house.' His mouth quirked. 'Paid them a small fortune to do this in as short a space of time as possible.'

Edie's chest swelled. 'You didn't have to go to all this trouble and expense.'

'I've asked you to be my guest for Christmas and I know you love it…'

Edie blinked rapidly and felt panicked, because tears were forming. She muttered something about needing the bathroom and escaped for a moment, locking the door behind her. She let the tears well and fall, pressing a hand to her mouth to stem any sound. Ridiculous to be so moved, but it was such a thoughtful gesture—and not the kind of thing she would have expected of a man like Sebastio at all. Especially when he hated Christmas so much.

When she felt composed again, and had splashed cold water on her face, she went back out and Sebastio was standing at the window.

He offered her a crystal glass when she came alongside him. 'Whisky?'

Edie nodded and hoped he wasn't suggesting she have some because he could see she'd been crying. She accepted the glass, taking a swift restorative sip before handing it back to him. It felt ridiculously intimate to share his whisky.

She kicked off her shoes, lowering her height a few precious inches. She said, 'For a man who doesn't like Christmas you fake it very well.'

He took a sip of the drink and looked at her. It was only now that she realised he'd taken off his jacket and undone his bow-tie and top button.

'I didn't always hate Christmas.'

She turned to face him. Intrigued. 'Really?'

He nodded, handing her the glass again. She held it.

'I used to spend Christmas with my maternal grand-mother—here in London, actually. My mother is half-English. My parents would leave me with her while they went on their annual Caribbean break.'

Edie listened as he told her about those few years when he'd experienced relative normality. He mentioned his grandmother's dog, a one-eyed rescue spaniel called Charlie.

He grimaced. 'When my grandmother died my parents refused to let me bring Charlie to Argentina. They had him put down.'

The thought of a young, *un*-cynical Sebastio, loving Christmas and his grandmother and a one-eyed dog, was too much for Edie to contain.

Her voice was husky. 'Your grandmother sounds like a lovely woman…and your parents were horrid to do that to her dog.'

'Believe me,' he said bitterly, 'that was the least of their sins.'

She had a very stark realisation then of how isolated he must have been. And how lucky she'd been to have had her modest but loving upbringing.

She handed him back the glass and he downed the drink. He put the glass down and faced Edie, an intent gleam in his eyes, turning them molten silver.

'I'm not really interested in talking right now.'

Feeling a sense of boldness creep over her under his explicit gaze, she said, 'What *are* you interested in?'

He tugged her towards him and turned her around, placing his big hands on her waist. She felt his breath and then his mouth on the bare skin at the back of her neck and then her shoulders as he drifted a trail of incendiary kisses along her skin.

Air touched her hot skin as he slowly drew the zip of her dress down. She knew she should care—she was standing right in front of a window—but it felt illicit and wonderful. She could see her reflection in the glass as the dress loosened and fell to her waist, revealing her strapless bra.

Sebastio pushed her dress down over her hips so that it fell to the floor. Edie knew she should care about that too, but she let it lie there at her feet. Sebastio came so close behind her she could feel his arousal through his clothes. He wound a hand around her front, spreading it possessively over her belly. Then he moved it up until he was cupping one lace-covered breast.

The tip tightened painfully against the lace and he pinched it gently, making her gasp. Then he whispered in her ear, 'I'm interested in making you fall apart, Edie.'

She was quivering like a taut bow. He undid her bra and peeled it away. She was naked now, except for her panties, and he made her watch their reflections in the window as he played her body like an instrument, until she was arching her back and his hand was deep between her legs, stroking her to a shattering orgasm.

She was so weak in the aftermath that he had to lift her up into his arms and take her straight into his bedroom, where he laid her down on the bed. He undressed with swift, graceful movements, and when he came down beside her on the bed Edie was already aching for him again.

She wondered with a mounting sense of desperation as he joined their bodies with a powerful thrust if she'd ever not want him with this insatiable hunger...

When Sebastio woke the following morning he put his hand out and frowned when it didn't touch Edie's warm sleeping body. He lifted his head and saw the room was empty. He felt a spurt of frustration as he got up and went to the adjoining door. He shouldn't have offered her another room.

But she wasn't there either.

He pulled on sweats and a top and went into the apartment. Dawn was coming up over the city, and when he saw Edie he felt a little breathless for a moment. She was sitting in one of his chairs, wearing a robe—his robe—and he could see that it drowned her.

She had her knees pulled up to her chin, her arms wrapped around them, and she was looking out of the window with a faint smile on her face. Her hair was messy and his hands itched to grab her up and carry her straight back to bed. For some reason he felt piqued that something private was making her smile.

But then she must have heard him because she looked around. 'Sorry, I didn't mean to wake you.'

He shook his head, coming into the room. 'You didn't.'

He was unable not to touch her, so he went over and plucked her up from the chair before sitting down and putting her on his lap.

She let out a surprised squeak and a chuckle. 'I was quite comfortable there, you know.'

'Now I bet you're even more comfortable.'

She blushed and Sebastio shook his head, tracing her jaw with a knuckle. 'Amazing how you can blush so easily after what we've just spent all night doing.'

She blushed even harder.

'What are you doing out here anyway?'

She shrugged. 'Just watching the city wake up. Christmas morning always feels magical to me. Like some kind of miracle has taken place overnight.' She ducked her head against his shoulder. 'You'll think I'm daft.'

He shook his head slowly. She'd put on the Christmas

tree lights and they sent out a low golden glow. It was the first time he'd ever had his own private space decorated for Christmas, and it reminded him of the Christmases he'd spent with his grandmother. For the first time since he'd bought this place it felt as if it had a little soul.

He said, 'I have a present for you.'

She tensed. 'But that's not fair. I had no time to do anything.'

Sebastio marvelled. Any other woman he'd ever been intimate with would be licking her lips and trying to hide the greedy gleam in her eyes.

He stood up, pulling Edie up with him, and took her over to the tree. He said ruefully, 'I'm afraid most of these boxes are empty—just dressing—but this one is for you.'

He handed her a small wrapped box and felt ridiculously self-conscious when she took it. He was very aware that she was naked under the robe. He could see the tantalising slope of one breast, the start of a dusky nipple...

She looked at him, biting her lip. 'You didn't have to do this.'

'Just open it, Edie,' he growled, not sure if he could control himself until she opened it.

Edie was all fingers and thumbs on the package. Her heart was tripping. She felt awful. Why hadn't she thought of getting Sebastio something? Even though she'd had no idea she'd be here? Once again he was surprising her.

The paper fell away to reveal a long rectangular black box. She opened it and sucked in a shaky breath. It was a stunning silver necklace with a perfectly formed teardrop diamond encased in platinum.

She looked up at Sebastio, darkly dangerous with his tousled hair and stubbled jaw. His actions had sent her into a spin, but she knew she shouldn't make anything of it because he must have done this a million times with other women. She desperately tried not to imbue it with any significance beyond a thoughtful gesure.

'I can't accept this—it's too much.'

He plucked the necklace out of the box and had it secured around her neck before she could stop him. For a man with big hands he was surprisingly dextrous. She put up a hand to feel it. The diamond nestled perfectly in the spot just below the little hollow at the centre of her collarbone.

'But I have nothing for you…'

He took her hand. 'You can come back to bed and show me your appreciation.' He smiled wickedly.

Much later that day, Sebastio revealed to Edie the Christmas feast that had been delivered and prepared by Fortnum & Mason staff. They dined on a traditional Christmas dinner with all the trimmings, and drank wine, still decadently dressed in their robes.

And as dusk fell over London once more Edie knew she'd just experienced a Christmas that would be etched into her memory for ever. The kind of Christmas she'd never imagined could be possible. She was deeply and irrevocably under Sebastio's magic spell. And she feared that it was way too late to try and save herself.

No matter what happened now, she would emerge from this experience emotionally bruised. More than bruised. But she knew she wouldn't have swapped it for anything. When the pain came—as it inevitably would—she would deal with it.

# CHAPTER EIGHT

'I want you to come to Argentina with me.'

Edie turned around from where she'd been looking out over the view of London. It was a view she thought she'd never get enough of. And it was a view that reminded her that while she was here in this glass cocoon high in the clouds with Sebastio it wasn't really *her* life. Her life was back on street level. Not up here. Even if during the past few idyllic, heady days she'd managed to block out the fact that reality was waiting in the wings.

Except maybe not just yet…

'Argentina?'

He nodded and pushed himself off the doorframe, where he'd been leaning nonchalantly. He was dressed in worn jeans and a loose shirt. How long had he been there? Watching her?

He came towards her with that effortless athletic grace, and predictably Edie's body responded. It was still sensitive after a night of passion that had left her feeling as weak as a kitten. She'd only just managed to drag herself out of bed, wash and eat something. More leftovers from their Christmas feast.

Sebastio had been on the phone in his office so she'd not disturbed him.

'I have to go to Buenos Aires for some meetings at the

bank and I've been invited to a New Year's party. Afterwards I could take you to my island for a couple of days.'

She remembered him mentioning it before. Santa Azul. It sounded impossibly exotic and out of her league. And it was, she told herself a little desperately.

She folded her arms, as if that could help block out Sebastio's intensely seductive pull. 'I would love to… But I can't just pick up and leave at a moment's notice.'

'Why not?'

His carefree attitude rubbed up against all the edgy bits inside her that told her she was a fool to have indulged herself like this here with him. 'Because life isn't that simple for all of us, Sebastio.'

He went still. 'I know very well that life isn't simple, Edie. I'm not suggesting it is. However, I won't apologise for the fact that I have resources available to me that can make things somewhat…easier.'

Edie felt chastened. He'd been nothing but generous. The necklace he'd given her nestled against her skin. She adored it, and hadn't taken it off since he'd put it around her neck. Even though she knew one of his assistants had probably picked it out.

'I'm sorry… I just don't think it would be a good idea.'

She dreaded him asking why, because in the fragile mood she was in right now she might blurt out the real reason. Because she was fathoms deep in love with him and struggling to stay afloat in a sea of emotions.

But he said, 'When are your parents due back from their cruise?'

She looked at him. 'Not till the third week in January.'

'And when are you due to return to work?'

'Helen hasn't contacted me yet with a return date.'

'So effectively you have no commitments at the moment?'

She shook her head, feeling her will to resist slipping away.

As if sensing her vacillation, Sebastio stepped closer. And then closer. She had no defence against him when he came within touching distance. And less than none when he touched her, sliding his hand around her neck, tugging her towards him. Bringing their bodies into contact.

'Come with me, Edie... I want to show you Buenos Aires and you'll love my island. We're not done, you and I. Not yet.'

*But we will be soon.*

He didn't have to say it.

The weak part of Edie reasoned logically that she was in so deep now, what could a few more days hurt? Sebastio made her feel vital and alive. Things she'd longed for so desperately at one time. Things she'd been afraid she'd never feel again. How could she turn her back on what he was offering?

Edie was curled into her seat, staring out of the plane's small window as they flew over the eastern coastline of Argentina and south to Buenos Aires. Sebastio's gaze ran over her figure. She was dressed in light trousers and a bright silk shirt with a bow at the neck that made his hands itch to undo it and slip the buttons out of their holes so he could—

He cursed silently.

What was it about this woman that still held him in her thrall? It was as if the more he got of her, the more insatiable he became. Her effect on him was growing, not waning. This had never happened to him with a woman before.

It was the only thing that was stopping him from dragging her to the back of the plane to make love to her. This clawing need to have her. It made him feel out of control. And yet it hadn't stopped him from bringing her with him.

She turned her head to look at him, as if she could hear his riotous thoughts. 'Why did you cut your hair so short?' he asked. 'It used to be longer.'

Edie immediately touched her hair self-consciously and she avoided his eye. He'd noticed she did that sometimes, and it made him want to tip her face to his so she couldn't hide from him.

'I just… It was more practical for work.'

Something niggled at Sebastio. He realised that for the first time since he'd met her he thought she was lying. Why would she lie about her hair, though?

She bent down and picked up a newspaper she'd been looking at earlier. She handed it over to Sebastio with a wary look on her face. 'Isn't this your friend who was in the car with you that night of the accident? It looks like he got married.'

Sebastio took the paper from Edie, frowning. He looked down and his breath caught in his throat.

It was a picture of Victor Sanchez. He was in his wheelchair and holding the hand of a woman who stood beside him, looking down at him and smiling broadly. She was very pretty, with dark hair in a fancy topknot, and a voluminous veil flowing behind her. She wore a white dress and held flowers in her other hand. Victor was wearing a suit with a flower in his buttonhole.

*Married.*

'They look very happy.'

Sebastio barely heard Edie's words above the roaring sound in his head. He skimmed the article…

*Miranda, who had been nursing Victor after the accident…fell in love…second chance of happiness after the horrific tragedy that claimed his wife and…*

Sebastio dropped the paper from his hand. All he could see was Victor's features, bruised and twisted with hatred and anger.

*'Damn you, Sebastio. You killed Maya and my baby. You ruined my life. You didn't deserve to survive. You're incapable of loving anyone... We had love. We had it all ahead of us and you took it away...'*

Sebastio was locked in the past and he only slowly became aware of Edie crouched next to him, her hand on his arm, while she put something small and cool in his other hand. He looked down stupidly to see a tumbler full of golden liquid. He lifted it and drank, allowing the alcohol to spread its warmth and restore his equilibrium.

'I'm sorry. I shouldn't have shown it to you... But I thought it might be a good thing.'

Sebastio curled his hand into a fist on his thigh. He needed to reach for Edie so badly right now that it scared him.

'I'm fine,' he gritted out.

He'd never been less fine.

She moved back and sat in her own seat. Sebastio took another sip of whisky. He could sense the question reverberating in her head. He could feel the weight of it.

Without her even asking, he said, 'It was my fault. The crash.'

'What happened?'

'We were on our way home from a match. Maya was in the back of the car. We were happy—we'd won. I took my attention off the road for a split-second and that was all it took. A drunk driver was on the wrong side of the road, coming straight for us. By the time I noticed, it was too late to swerve or do anything. It was a head-on collision. And yet I walked away with barely a scratch.

'Victor was paralysed from the waist down. He'd been

one of the world's best rugby full-backs and had just signed a contract with one of the biggest clubs in Europe. Maya was half-French—they were due to go to Paris, to live there for a few years.'

Sebastio's voice was toneless, but Edie could hear the underlying emotion. She bitterly regretted showing him the article now. She'd only been trying to distract him from asking her about her hair. When he'd gone so pale she'd acted on instinct to get him something for shock…

'Maya was thrown from the car. She and her baby died almost instantly.'

The bleakness in Sebastio's voice scored at Edie's heart. 'I can't imagine what that must have been like…to experience such a tragedy.'

*Except she could.*

She'd watched people she'd become close to die while she'd survived. So she did know how Sebastio felt on some level.

He said, 'They had everything going for them. They'd only been married a year and they were about to have a baby, a whole new life in France…'

'But it wasn't your fault. The other driver had been drinking—'

Sebastio's focus snapped back to her. 'If I hadn't been distracted I would have seen him coming… I could have swerved, or done something… Victor was right to blame me.'

At that moment an air steward appeared and informed them they'd be landing shortly. Edie secured her belt and glanced at Sebastio, who was looking out of his window broodingly.

She wanted to say more but she bit her lip. The weight of Sebastio's guilt hung heavy in the space between them. No wonder it was so acute if his own friend had blamed him. The worst of it was how badly she wanted to be able to do something to assuage his pain. Reassure him it hadn't been his fault. But he seemed determined to blame himself.

She forced herself to look away, out of her own window. Sebastio's pain wasn't her responsibility. She couldn't afford to let herself get any more invested.

But as the plane touched down with a screech of tyres she knew it was futile. She was already invested. Beyond all hope.

By the time they were driving through the city in a chauffeur-driven Jeep Edie was already transfixed by the majesty and beauty of Buenos Aires.

She looked at Sebastio as she buzzed her window down. 'Do you mind?'

He shrugged and smiled and she was relieved to see that intense brooding expression replaced by something else. He might have had a tragic experience here, and a not-so-happy childhood, but it was clear he loved this city. He looked relaxed in a way she'd never seen before, his dark good looks complemented by the vibrant surroundings.

Edie's eyes couldn't take it all in fast enough as they drove down wide boulevards and she looked up at the soaring elegant buildings. They were entering an area with wide leafy streets and even more elegant buildings now. Edie didn't know much about archictecture, but some of the houses reminded her of pictures she'd seen of Paris.

There were manicured parks, with children playing by fountains and old men sitting in groups talking. It was refined and exotic and a world away from grey and cold London.

They drew to a stop on a quiet street that bordered one of the parks. Sebastio helped her out and immediately she felt overdressed and too hot in the silk shirt and trousers.

Summer in the southern hemisphere was intense, even in the late afternoon.

A very beautiful woman walked past with a perfectly groomed poodle and Edie felt a bubble of pure joy rise up. She'd never in a million years have experienced this if it wasn't for Sebastio.

She turned to him impulsively before they walked into the building. 'Thank you for this... I love it.'

His mouth quirked. 'We've only just arrived.'

She refused to feel embarrassed at her own gaucheness. 'I know...but still, thank you.'

Sebastio watched Edie walk into the foyer of his apartment building—he owned the entire building—and saw the effect of her smile on the concierge. He scowled at the man and led Edie into the lift, and up to his floor. The top floor.

Her words came back to him. *'You really couldn't care less, could you?'* But the problem was that he did care. He'd just made an art out of pretending not to.

But seeing Victor's picture in that paper earlier... His friend's happiness had impacted Sebastio deeply—the man had lost everything and yet he obviously still had the capacity to love and seek joy.

Sebastio saw Edie out on the terrace that wrapped around the front of his apartment and welcomed the distraction from his brooding thoughts. He shrugged off his jacket and went to join her, pushing aside everything in his head except for *her* and indulging in this crazy chemistry.

It was part of the reason he'd asked her to come—because with a sense of something bordering on desperation he fully expected her appeal to wane, sooner rather than later... But not yet. He pressed close behind her, sliding his arms around her slim waist.

Edie put her hands on Sebastio's over her belly. She felt

the strangest sensation for a moment, light-headed, and gripped his arms tight as if she might fall.

He tensed. 'Are you okay?'

It passed as quickly as it had come and Edie nodded. 'Just hungry, probably. I should have eaten more on the plane.'

'We'll go out for some food, but first...'

Sebastio turned her around so her back was to the terrace wall and she was looking up at him. As stunning as Buenos Aires was, she knew which view she'd choose.

He pressed close. 'How hungry are you?'

She felt his erection pressing into her soft flesh. Her body and mind melted. 'Ravenous.'

She reached up and drew him down, touching her mouth to his, savouring the moment and the man, storing up every precious second like a miser.

'Where are you now?'

'In the cemetery, looking for Eva Peron's grave.'

Sebastio smiled, imagining Edie with a frown on her face as she looked at the map.

'Just follow the rest of the tourists—that's probably the easiest way to find it.'

Last night, after they'd gone out for something to eat—very late—Edie had given him something in a bag and said shyly, 'It's just something silly. I never got you a Christmas present.'

Sebastio could still remember the tight feeling in his chest when he'd opened the bag and taken out a small furry toy dog. Edie had customised it with an eye-patch.

She'd said, 'I know it probably doesn't look anything like your grandmother's dog, but maybe he'll do until you get a dog of your own one day.'

Sebastio had been gobsmacked. First of all, no woman

had ever given him a gift. And secondly, the chances of him ever getting a dog had always been somewhere between nil and zero. But suddenly, for a shimmering second before he'd been able to shut it down, the possibility had existed. Somewhere in the future.

The gesture had been incredibly sweet, and instead of making Sebastio feel claustrophobic, or like running a mile, it had only made him want her more.

He heard the low buzz of voices behind him and turned back to see a long table full of his diligent employees. His chief of staff was near the head of the table, and he looked at his watch and then at Sebastio expressively.

He was one of the few people Sebastio had kept on from his father's days to help keep the transition smooth and Sebastio decided he'd now served his purpose. No one told him what to do.

He said to Edie, 'Stay where you are. I'll come and meet you.'

'But how will you find me?'

'Trust me. I'll find you.' She stood out like a beacon in Buenos Aires, with her pale skin and bright auburn hair.

Sebastio adjourned the meeting, telling his employees to take the rest of the day off and that he didn't expect to see them until after the New Year. Then he took his chief of staff aside and informed him that he would be giving the man his notice and a very healthy severance package in the New Year.

When he walked out of the bank and got into the back of his car he felt truly light for the first time in a long time.

Edie knew Sebastio was coming to meet her, but she was still unprepared to see him striding through the magnificent and imposing mausoleum gravestones of Recoleta Cemetery with his jacket off, hooked over his shoulder by a finger, and his other hand in his pocket. Her heart went wild and she heard a collective appreciative gasp go up from a group of female tourists from America nearby.

He stopped in front of her and he was dazzling. Never more so than in this place which commemorated the dead. His vitality was intoxicating.

'Did you pay your respects to Evita?'

Edie nodded, giddy that he'd come to spend time with her.

He said, 'Good.' And then he took her hand and led her away.

They spent the afternoon wandering around the local colourful districts. She loved exploring the wide streets, and almost cried when they stopped to watch a couple of street performers dance a tango to the most melancholic, soulful music she'd ever heard.

She caught Sebastio rolling his eye and muttering something like *'Tourists...'* under his breath and she punched him in the arm.

He responded by stopping and kissing her very thoroughly in the middle of the street, much to the appreciation of the passing crowd. Someone even threw a coin their way.

Edie's face was still flaming after that very unexpected public display of affection when he took her into a very exclusive-looking boutique down a side street.

She caught his arm, whispering, 'What are you doing?'

He said, 'Remember I mentioned a party? Well, it's a New Year's Eve party being thrown by friends of mine at their house tomorrow evening. You'll need a dress.'

Immediately Edie's bubble burst a little. It was one thing spending time alone with Sebastio, but another thing entirely actually meeting his peers. *Friends.* She wasn't one of them.

He seemed to read her mind and tipped her chin up so she had to look at him. 'They're nice people. I promise.'

Edie smiled weakly, just as a stunningly beautiful dark-haired woman approached and spoke in rapid Spanish to Sebastio. Edie was whisked away before she could protest, and when she looked back he was sitting on a wide chair, being handed a newspaper and a cup of coffee by another equally beautiful assistant.

For a moment something icy trickled down her spine. It was obviously a scenario he was used to, because he looked as at home here as he did in his apartment. And evidently the staff knew him from before. Him and his lovers.

As the women fussed around Edie she told herself she shouldn't be feeling hurt. This was just a timely reminder of how finite this all was.


Sebastio's levels of arousal were dangerously high by the time Edie emerged from the dressing room in yet another dress. So he almost exploded when he saw the very short, thigh-skimming dark blue sequinned dress. On anyone else it might have looked cheap. Tacky. But Edie's innate elegance and long slim legs elevated it to a couture gown.

It had a high neck and elbow-length sleeves, so it was positively demure on top—apart from the fact that it clung to her body like a second skin and showed off her slender curves and the high, firm thrust of her breasts.

'We'll take it—and all the others,' Sebastio said, sounding slightly strangled.

Edie looked shocked. 'Sebastio, that is really not necessary—'

He stood up and ignored her, instructing the sales assistant to pack up all the dresses before paying.

When Edie was dressed in her own jeans and T-shirt again—which felt like rags compared to the dresses she'd been trying on—she came out of the dressing room to find Sebastio's driver had somehow miraculously appeared and was carrying out what looked like hundreds of bags. Sebastio must have bought even more clothes.

She turned to Sebastio outside the shop. 'First of all, thank you—you're being far too generous. But that was really unnecessary. I don't need all those clothes—where would I even wear them?'

Suddenly Edie couldn't read his expression and it made her nervous. He put his sunglasses on, hiding his eyes. 'Do with them what you will, Edie. They're a gift.'

Of course. It was no big deal because he'd done this before. They were just clothes to decorate his latest lover and he was a billionaire so he could afford it.

The thing that bothered Edie most, though, as Sebastio helped her into the back of his car, was that she didn't want to be like his other women...

The following evening Edie was nervous as they approached the grand and imposing entrance to Sebastio's friends' house, which wasn't far from his apartment.

He'd told her that the host had been one of his closest companions growing up. He was married and had two children. So when they got to the door and she saw a gorgeous couple—him, tall and arrestingly dark and handsome in a classic tuxedo, and her, exquisitely pretty with dark eyes and russet-brown hair caught up in a chignon—both smiling widely, something inside Edie eased.

They looked nice. Intimidatingly gorgeous, but nice.

'Edie, I'd like you to meet Rafael and Isobel Romero.'

Isobel came forward, smiling warmly, stunning in a long sequinned black gown. 'Edie, I'm so pleased to meet you. Thank you for coming.'

Edie smiled. 'Nice to meet you too.'

Rafael introduced himself too, placing an arm firmly around his wife's waist after they'd done their introductions. It was only then that Edie noticed the neat but very definite bump under Isobel's form-fitting dress.

The other woman noticed Edie's look and grimaced, saying sotto voce, 'I really need to work out my timings better. Being pregnant at the height of an Argentinian summer is not very clever, but somehow I've managed to do it every time.'

Edie's eyes widened. 'You sound English.'

'My father was English, and I spent a lot of time in England. By the way, I love your hair. Mine used to be that short too, and I'm seriously considering getting it cut again—it's so much easier to manage.'

Her husband interrupted them with a growl. 'No, you're not.' He looked at Edie. 'No offence—your hair is beautiful—but I prefer my wife's hair long.'

Isobel rolled her eyes, but Edie could see a look of teasing and something much hotter pass between them. She felt a pang of envy at their obvious affection, and just then two small blurs collided with them. A girl of about eight—a mini-me of her mother, with dark hair and eyes—and a little boy of about five. A handsome replica of his father.

Inexplicably Edie felt a lurch in her gut. A sudden hollow sensation. She'd always known that children most likely wouldn't be a part of her future, but she'd never felt it so keenly before. It was disconcerting to be feeling this here, now, with Sebastio standing at her side. A man who would run a mile from the mere suggestion of family.

Rafael and Isobel introduced them to the children, Beatriz and Luis, who were hopping with excitement at the prospect of fireworks later, and then efficiently dispatched them with their nannies while showing Sebastio and Edie through to the party so they could greet the other guests now arriving.

The sheer opulence of the event made Edie's head spin. It was being held in a huge marquee in the gorgeous land-scaped back garden, lit with a thousand fairy lights. It made her Christmas dressing skills feel very inadequate.

The house was situated on a hill, so there was a spec-tacular view of the city all the way to the port, where the last rays of the setting blood-red sun were staining the sky. England and its blizzards and winter seemed very far away.

Sebastio looked at Edie. Her eyes were huge. He'd had to physically restrain himself from clamping her to his side in front of Rafael—it had shocked him how suddenly posses-sive he'd felt, even though he knew his friend was deeply besotted with his wife. But he'd noticed his friend look at Edie speculatively, and he knew it was because she wasn't like the women Sebastio had brought as dates in the past. He'd felt exposed.

But now any sense of exposure was fast being eclipsed by the fact that Edie was effortlessly drawing lots of lin-gering glances, with her endless pale legs and lithe body. Sebastio regretted buying her the dress now, even though other women there were even more scantily clad.

He gave in to the possessive surge rushing through him and snaked an arm around her waist, turning her so that she was facing him. Looking up. All he could see were those huge blue eyes and long lashes. That provocative mouth that never said what he expected.

He bent his head and crushed her mouth under his, kiss-ing her deeply.

When he pulled back he noted with satisfaction that it took a second for her to open her eyes, and when she did they were unfocused.

'What was that for?' she asked, sounding dazed.

*What had that been for?* asked a mocking voice inside Sebastio's head.

He was losing it. He'd never felt the need to stamp his claim on a woman before. And yet he couldn't stop the honest truth from tripping out of his mouth. 'Because I can't *not* kiss you when you look at me like that.'

Edie really wished he wouldn't do this. Make her heart flutter with a very dangerous sense of hope. Because it didn't mean anything. Nor did the fact that she was his first lover in four years. None of it meant anything. All he meant was that he wanted her. Pure physical chemistry. Not emotion.

But by the time the fireworks were illuminating the Buenos Aires sky after midnight Edie was glad she was sitting on the grass between Sebastio's legs, her back against his chest, so he wouldn't see the tears welling in her eyes at the beauty of it all.

It wasn't only the spectacular fireworks taking her attention, though, as Isobel and Rafael Romero were nearby, each holding a wonderstruck child in their arms. A unit of love and family. Edie's belly actually ached this time, and she put a hand to it, biting her lip to stem the tide of emotion.

Sebastio's voice came, near to her ear. 'Okay?'

She nodded rapidly, terrified he'd see something of the turmoil she felt.

'Ready to leave?' Sebastio's voice was rough and loaded with intent.

His hand snaked around and rested over hers on her belly. She could feel his body stirring at her back and closed her eyes at the inevitable response, making her ready for him. Making her needy. Desperate. Craving.

She nodded and whispered, 'Yes…let's go.'

In the car on the way back to his apartment the sexual

tension was thick enough to cut with a knife. By the time they were in the lift Sebastio had pressed Edie against the wall and was kissing her as if his life depended on it.

She didn't remember leaving the lift and entering the apartment, or getting to the bedroom. All she knew was that she needed to be joined with Sebastio or she would die. Her need was that acute.

He thrust deep and hard, bringing her leg up so that he went even deeper. Edie closed her eyes but he said, 'Open them… Edie, look at me.'

She did, and as he forced her to connect with him on every level, allowing her no quarter, she cursed him silently even as she fell apart into a million pieces.

Two days later Edie was looking out of another plane window, at a small island covered in green in the middle of the ocean. Waves lapped against white sand beaches and palm trees swayed in the breeze.

It was pretty much your quintessential tropical island paradise. There was a huge colonial-style house in the centre of the island, and Edie could make out a path leading from the house to the beach. There were smaller buildings in a cluster near the main house, and she guessed those must be for staff.

The plane landed and she saw a man waiting with an open-top Jeep to drive them to the house. Sebastio greeted the driver warmly and after introducing him to Edie got into the back.

When they were driving along the road, Edie couldn't help observing, 'You never drive. You don't like to, or…?' She stopped, suddenly aghast at what she'd just said. How insensitive it had been.

Sebastio's jaw clenched. He looked at her. 'I haven't driven since that night.'

'I'm sorry. I didn't mean to—'

He shook his head, negating her apology and shutting the conversation down.

The knot that had been in Edie's belly since the party intensified. Unconsciously she placed a hand there. She'd been feeling all over the place since meeting Rafael and Isobel. Seeing how happy they were, seeing their children, had touched on something very vulnerable in Edie. She'd never really articulated to herself how devastated she'd been to learn that she might not ever have a family…and it had hit her forcibly that night.

Then, when they'd returned to the apartment…when they'd made love…it had felt so much more intense than at any other time. Edie had felt flayed afterwards. It had been as if a layer of civility had been stripped away between her and Sebastio, exposing something far more raw and visceral.

The following day she hadn't woken until the afternoon. She hadn't been able to put her finger on it but she'd felt… *off*, somehow.

Immediately alarm bells had rung. She was hyper-conscious of anything changing in her health since the cancer. After all, she'd only found out about that because she'd felt an innocuous lump in her neck and had gone to get it checked out.

So she'd rung her GP back in Britain, and as a result of that conversation had gone to a pharmacy to buy a pregnancy test. Now it was sitting in her luggage like a ticking time bomb.

Her GP had reminded her that the chances of her getting pregnant were very slim, but had suggested that they rule it out first, just to be safe.

Edie hadn't had the nerve to do the test before they'd left Buenos Aires, not ready to face the enormity of what the result might mean. The thought that she might be pregnant absolutely terrified Edie, and filled her with euphoria at the same time.

It would be the ultimate test of her health. To know that she could create a life after almost losing hers. After being pumped full of toxins. But for it to happen like this…? With a man who had expressly told her he didn't do relationships or commitment…?

'Are you okay? You look like you've seen a ghost.'

Edie forced a smile and looked at Sebastio. 'Fine…just a little tired.'

'You can rest when we get to the house. I have some work calls to make, just to make sure everything is running smoothly for the next few days.'

Edie's thoughts immediately went to the box in the white paper bag in her luggage. She felt clammy. 'Okay.'

When they got to the house she was too tense to really notice how stunning it was. But it *was* stunning. Set amongst lush vegetation. Totally cut off from the outside world. A wide veranda surrounded the lower floor and there was a huge pool in the manicured back garden, with views of the sea beyond.

It was paradise.

The rooms were large and airy, doors and windows open to let the breeze flow through. Edie was wearing a white broderie anglaise sundress and even that felt too hot in the sultry heat.

A beautiful woman appeared, holding a tray with refreshing drinks. Sebastio introduced her as Angelique. Edie smiled her thanks and savoured the tart lemon juice.

The bedroom was massive. Wooden floorboards and white muslin drapes flowing in the breeze. Open shutters and French doors leading out to a balcony where the view took in the sea and, in the very far distance, the coastline of Argentina.

Sebastio felt an inordinate amount of satisfaction to see Edie here. Her back was to him, pale and slender in her dress. Her neck looked fragile. He felt a spurt of something very alien—protectiveness.

He'd never brought another woman here. This was his place, where he'd come after the accident. Where he'd been raw and broken. Where he'd endured long days and where his thoughts had got very dark. Days he didn't like to remember.

Maybe that was why he'd brought her here? To eclipse those memories? Maybe finally it was time.

And the fact that he'd done it told him that she was different. That maybe she had a place in his life.

The thought of letting Edie go sent a tendril of panic through him. Not a pleasant sensation. But perhaps he didn't have to let her go… Although he'd never taken a mistress before…

She turned around at that moment, as if sensing his circling thoughts, and immediately he wanted her. He could see the faint outline of her breasts under the thin dress. The curve of her waist.

He went over and put his hands either side of her body. He bent down and relished that split second before his mouth touched hers…and then the way she responded with such sweet sensuality.

He pulled back, his blood humming. He wanted nothing more than to take her over to the bed but she did look tired. And pale.

'Have a shower and a nap, Edie. I'll wake you later, when dinner is ready.'

She smiled. 'That sounds like a good idea.'

Edie's smile faded as she watched Sebastio walk out of

the room. The driver of the Jeep—Pedro—had just delivered their luggage and she went over to hers, taking out the pharmacy bag.

She went into the bathroom and locked the door, barely noticing the white marbled luxuriousness.

She wasn't sure how much time passed before she had the nerve to do the test. And then there was more waiting as she sat on the closed toilet seat.

After the allotted time Edie picked up the test and held her breath as she read the result.

*Where was she?*

Sebastio felt a spurt of frustration as he searched for Edie. She wasn't in the bedroom, sleeping. She wasn't downstairs.

He went upstairs again and checked the bathroom. No sign.

He was about to leave when he saw a white paper bag in the bin. Without even knowing why it had caught his attention he bent down to pick it up and something fell out…

# CHAPTER NINE

EDIE STOOD ON the edge of the sea and felt the waves lap at her feet. She didn't even remember leaving the bathroom or coming down here. She'd gravitated here instinctively, in shock. Reeling.

*She was pregnant.*

She couldn't deny she felt panicked, because this was hardly the ideal situation in which to be pregnant.

But all she could think of was what her doctor had said. *'If you are pregnant, Edie, then it's is a very good sign. It means your body has recovered from the treatment and your fertility hasn't been irreparably damaged.'*

She put her hands on her belly. Hard to believe there was a little kernel of life growing inside her right now. But here was the proof that she was well and a miracle of sorts had happened.

*New life.*

She would have to tell Sebastio, of course. And she dreaded his reaction. But just for now, for this private moment, she would allow the pure joy she felt to suffuse her whole body. No matter what happened, she would love and care for this baby. Even if she had to do it on her own.

A fierce wave of love and protectiveness washed through her. She couldn't stop smiling.

'Happy with yourself, are you?' Sebastio's voice was like the lash of a whip it was so cold.

Edie whirled around, her smile fading. She'd never seen Sebastio look so angry. But it was a contained, cold anger. He was holding something in his hand.

The test. With that one word: *Embarazada.*

It was the Spanish word for pregnant. She'd looked it up before she'd done the test.

'Sebastio… I just found out… I didn't have any idea.'

'You told me that you couldn't get pregnant. You told me something had happened to you.'

Edie felt sick at the bitterly accusing tone in his voice. She had. And she couldn't keep the truth from him now.

'Something did happen to me. I wasn't lying… The chances were so slim…' She trailed off. Evidently not slim enough.

Sebastio was shaking his head. 'I have been such an idiot. Blinded by lust. I should never have believed you. I should have listened to my gut when it told me your act of innocence was just that. But I will admit that faking your virginity was a master move.'

Edie's mouth opened in shock. 'I *was* a virgin.'

But Sebastio was hardly listening to her. 'The way you stopped and told me… Of course all I could think about was how much I wanted you. And then you came to me, re-member? You *asked* me to make love to you. Begged me.'

Edie's face flamed with shame. She had asked him. She had gone to him with every atom of her courage and asked him to take her innocence. And now he was twisting it.

'It wasn't like that,' she whispered.

'We are not staying here. Be ready to leave in half an hour.'

Sebastio had turned and was striding away, back up the path, before Edie could move.

She went after him. 'Sebastio, *wait*.'

He stopped. His tall body rigid with rejection. He turned around. 'Yes? More lies?'

Edie refused to let him intimidate her. 'What about the baby?'

He flicked a cold glance to her belly and then back up to her face. 'First of all I will have it confirmed by a doctor that you are in fact pregnant, and then, assuming that it's mine until such time as we can disprove that, I will make all the necessary arrangements.'

Edie just heard 'necessary arrangements' and went icy.

She put a hand on her belly. 'I am not getting rid of this baby.'

Sebastio's mouth curled. 'That is not what I meant. If there is a baby and it is mine, then it will be afforded my full protection.'

*If. It.*

The words landed like barbs all over Edie's skin. Sebastio had turned and was walking away again. She was rooted to the spot. A block of ice. He was suggesting it mightn't even be his. The thought made a semi-hysterical giggle bubble up inside Edie. But she was too shocked to let it out.

She forced her legs to move and followed Sebastio back into the house.

Within the space of an hour, her world had come tumbling down and it was so much worse than she'd thought it might be.

Sebastio had retreated to a place of icy numb control during the journey back to Buenos Aires. He'd been acutely aware of Edie beside him, but he hadn't been able to look at her. The sense of betrayal he'd felt when he'd picked up that plastic stick and realised what he was looking at was huge and it still reverberated inside him.

He'd spent his first Christmas in four years with another person. He'd brought her to Argentina. He'd walked out of an important meeting because it had seemed more important to spend time with her. He'd brought her to the island—his sanctuary.

What had she done to him? Who had he become? Not someone he recognised.

After a lifetime of adhering to a self-protecting code of cynicism he'd suddenly reverted to a place of blind trust? He'd even been contemplating making her a more permanent fixture in his life…when all along she'd had a far more ambitious game-plan.

*She was pregnant.*

The thought made a cold sweat break out over his skin. He'd already been responsible for the deaths of a mother and child. How on earth could he hope to nurture and protect a defenceless baby? He'd always vowed never to have children, not wanting to put any child through what his parents had put him through. And that vow had solidified after the crash.

Yet if she *was* pregnant, and it *was* his—

His heart stopped at a sudden unbidden image of a tiny dark-haired infant suckling at Edie's breast. *Damn.* Enough. He would provide for the child, obviously, but he couldn't contemplate anything further than that right now.

They'd just walked back into his apartment when Edie said, 'Sebastio, I need to tell you something.'

He steeled himself, feeling an almost superstitious aversion to looking at her, as if that might unravel the fierce control he was exerting over himself.

*He can't even look at me*, Edie thought, sickened.

She refused to let him treat her as if she was invisible, though, and she put down her bag and walked around him so she stood in front of him.

Those silver-grey eyes blazed down into hers. For a fleeting moment Edie had the sensation that if he felt this much anger then surely it had to mean strong emotions were at play and maybe there was a chance she could appeal to him…

'I wasn't lying when I told you I had my reasons for believing I couldn't get pregnant.'

'It's too late for excuses.'

'It's not an excuse.' Edie's voice was sharp. She was on edge after the overload of tension and Sebastio's icy dismissal of her.

Sebastio stood still. Not moving away.

She swallowed. 'I had cancer when I was in my teens. A rare type of lymphoma. I went through months of chemotherapy and radiation. One area that was specifically targeted was my uterus, which is why the prospect of my getting pregnant was so slim. Slim enough for me to believe it wouldn't happen.'

He said nothing.

She continued. 'The night I saw you…the night in the club… I'd just been given the all-clear. I was wearing a wig.' She touched her hair self-consciously. 'That's why it was longer. I had no hair after the chemo. And I haven't let it grow long since then because I have a superstitious fear that if I do the cancer will come back.' She stopped, her heart thumping painfully.

Sebastio looked totally expressionless. He looked like a different person. Remote. Austere. Like he had that night in the club when he'd told her to *run along*.

Eventually he said, 'If this is true, why didn't you tell me before?'

*'If this is true.'*

The pain of him not believing her almost blindsided Edie for a moment. 'It is true.' She pulled down her top and touched her port scar. 'This is where they fed the drugs into my system.'

He barely flicked a glance down.

She went on. 'The reason I didn't tell you was because I didn't want you to think of me as fragile...vulnerable. I didn't want you to remember me like that. It was a tough time. I prefer not to think about it.'

And yet he had told her almost everything, Sebastio realised bitterly. More than he'd ever told anyone else.

He was aware of the faint red line under her collarbone, and he didn't like to think that it had allowed toxins to be fed into her system, but once again the jury was out on whether or not this was just an elaborate ruse to gain his sympathy.

He'd be a fool to fall for it.

He looked at his watch and said, 'I've arranged an appointment with my physician tomorrow morning. We'll discuss what happens next after that. I'm going to go into the office now and I won't be back until late tonight.'

In other words, she was dismissed.

Edie said nothing as Sebastio walked out of the apartment again. A wave of weariness came over her and she went into the bedroom that she hadn't yet used and climbed under the covers, willing sleep to come and mute the pain she was feeling.

Edie had elected not to have Sebastio in the doctor's office with her the following morning, but when she emerged the doctor came with her to meet him. He confirmed that Edie was indeed in the very early stages of pregnancy. About three weeks. As he said this to Sebastio Edie felt her cheeks grow hot, realising that they must have conceived that first time they'd made love.

Sebastio's reaction to the doctor was as stony-faced as

it had been to her for the past twenty-four hours. He just said, 'Okay, let's go.'

In the car on the way back to the apartment Edie said tautly, 'I did not pretend to be a virgin and this baby *is* yours.'

Sebastio looked at her and for a second she thought she saw a flicker of emotion before it disappeared. She knew this news was as much of a shock to him as it was to her, but right now she wasn't in any mood to compensate for his shock. Or his distrust.

When they got back to the apartment Edie went straight to her room and packed her bag, leaving behind everything Sebastio had given her. She just wanted to leave this place now. Go back to familiar surroundings, lick her wounds and think about what she was going to do. How she was going to cope. She wasn't prepared to put up with Sebastio's cold condemnation a moment longer.

When she came out he was standing at the window. He turned around and frowned. 'Where do you think you're going?'

'I'm going home.'

'I'm not returning to London until next week. I have meetings lined up here.'

'That's got nothing to do with me, Sebastio. We can talk about things when you come to London, but right now I'm leaving.'

She turned and walked to the door, but a hand landed on it right in front of her face. 'How do you think you're going to get there?'

She stepped back and looked fixedly at the door. 'I'll get a cab to the airport and take the next flight to England. There's bound to be one soon.'

'Don't be ridiculous. You could be waiting for two days. You'll stay here until I leave and we can go together.'

She looked at him. 'Am I a prisoner now?'

'Of course not. But you are pregnant with my baby—' He sounded exasperated.

'Oh, so you're willing to concede that much now?' Edie realised how on edge she was when she heard the jeering tone in her voice. She'd never spoken to anyone like this before.

Sebastio said nothing for a long moment and then, 'You really want to go home right now? Today?'

She nodded. Not trusting herself to speak.

Sebastio took his hand from the door and said coolly, 'Then I will organise it for you. Just give me ten minutes.'

Within twenty minutes Edie was in the back of his car heading towards the private airfield where his plane was waiting. Sebastio sat beside her, drumming his fingers on his thigh. It only made her tension increase.

When they got to the airfield he took her suitcase on board and said, 'Paolo and the staff will see you safely home. I will return in a few days. I have arranged for you to be taken directly to my apartment.'

Edie opened her mouth to object, but Sebastio put up a hand.

'Please, do not argue with me. Until we discuss what is going to happen you are under my protection. This isn't just about us any more.'

Edie swallowed a ball of emotion. *There never had been an us.*

It just went to show how little Sebastio had cared for her that he found it so easy to cast her aside. Anger welled up, drowning the other dangerous emotions. She couldn't believe she'd allowed herself to hope for anything in those fleeting moments when she'd thought she'd seen something in his eyes. Yet she could still feel the ever-present awareness and sexual tension simmering between them in spite of everything.

It galvanised her into saying, 'What about us…?'

'Everything is different now.'

'Because I'm not some disposable lover any more? Because I've had the temerity to fall pregnant?'

'I told you right from the start that I was not interested in commitment or a relationship. You were under no illusions.'

He was so cold he scared Edie, but she refused to let him see it. 'I know. But sometimes things happen outside of our control…'

He shook his head. 'Not in my world. I will deal with this consequence of our actions, but what we had is over, Edie.'

A few days later, back in London, in Sebastio's penthouse, the pain of his parting words had faded to a dull ache. The worst of it was that, knowing about his life and what he'd been through, Edie had some perspective on why he was shutting her out so comprehensively. It didn't excuse his behaviour, though, or make it any easier to bear.

When she'd landed back in London she'd had every intention of going back to her own apartment, but she'd been met by the resistance of Sebastio's driver, Nick, and one of his assistants, who'd come to meet her and told her firmly that they had instructions to take her to his apartment and see that she had everything she needed.

She'd given in eventually, after asking Nick to take her to her apartment first so she could collect some things.

Sebastio was right. It wasn't just about them now. It was about the baby, and she would at least do as he asked until they spoke when he came back. Which was any minute now. He'd been due to land about an hour ago.

Edie still wasn't prepared to see him. When she heard

the main door opening and closing she turned around from the window, arms folded. Tense all over.

Sebastio walked into the room, his eyes zeroing in on her immediately. She felt it like a jolt of electricity running through her system.

'You're here,' he said flatly.

Edie nodded. He came into the room and Edie could see that he looked slightly strained. Her gut clenched. Did he really hate her so much?

'I'm never sure what to expect where you're concerned.'

Edie flinched inwardly. 'I didn't intend for this to happen, no matter what you might believe. It truly was a minute chance that I could get pregnant.'

'*If* what you say about your cancer is true.'

Edie went cold all over. 'You still don't believe me.'

Sebastio was expressionless. Bored, even. 'I believe that people will go to extraordinary lengths to seek a lifetime of security. You've hit the jackpot with pregnancy.'

Edie put a hand to her belly. It was trembling. 'This is *your* baby. Our baby. It wasn't conceived out of nefarious intentions. He, or she, was conceived out of l—' She stopped herself just in time.

Sebastio's eyes narrowed. He sneered. 'What were you going to say? *Love?*' He imbued the word with extreme distaste. 'There was no love involved, Edie. Just lust.'

Edie couldn't do it. She couldn't pretend to be impervious like him. Cold and cynical.

She lifted her chin. 'There *is* love—on my side anyway. I love you, Sebastio, in spite of doing my best not to fall for you. That's why I left before the last party. To get away. I knew then that if I let the affair continue I'd get hurt. But it was too late even then…'

Sebastio heard Edie's words but they didn't—couldn't—impact on the impenetrable wall he'd constructed around himself in the last few days. In spite of that, though, his last image before going to sleep every night had been her stricken face when he'd left her on his plane. And every night since she'd left he'd had that nightmare about the crash. Waking sweating and cursing. His body slick with sweat, aching for Edie's soothing touch. Damn her.

And now she was looking at him with those wide deep blue eyes and telling him she loved him.

The words of his ex-lover came back to him. *'Women will tell you they love you but it doesn't exist. Not for us... They will only want you for your success and your wealth...'*

'Please,' he said, 'save yourself the dramatics. Your future is assured, thanks to your pregnancy. You'll never want for anything, nor will the baby.'

Edie absorbed the fact that he'd just thrown her admission of love back in her face. 'I get it,' she said.

'Get what?'

'Why you can't believe me. How can someone who grew up with parents who used him as a pawn even know what love looks like or feels like?'

'Edie...'

There was clear warning in Sebastio's voice but she ignored it. 'You don't believe you deserve it. How can you when your own friend blamed you for a tragedy that wasn't your fault? Victor shouldn't have blamed you. You were as much a victim of that awful accident as they were. You deserve to be happy too. You've been punishing yourself for too long.'

The bones on his face stood out starkly and he stalked over to where Edie was standing. She refused to take a step back. Tension snapped between them. She felt the heat. She could see it in Sebastio's eyes. But he resented it. She could see that too.

'You think it's that simple? That all I need to do is forgive myself and forget a lifetime of lessons to trust in an emotion that is as intangible to me as air?'

She felt reckless. She stepped up to him, toe to toe. She grabbed his hand and held it over her thumping heart. 'Is that tangible enough for you? My heart is *yours*, Sebastio, whether you want it or not.'

He emitted a foreign word that sounded like a curse and curled a hand behind Edie's neck. His mouth crashed down on hers before she had time to prepare.

Who was she kidding? She'd never have time to prepare for Sebastio.

She was engulfed in heat and want and need. It was so acute she let out a little moan.

Sebastio tore his mouth off hers and stepped back. Edie almost fell forward, totally disorientated for a moment.

'You're wrong,' he said harshly. 'That's the only tangible thing I'm interested in.'

Edie didn't trust herself to speak. She'd already said enough. So when Sebastio turned on his heel and walked out she was almost relieved, because she needed privacy to absorb the bleak reality that there truly was no way she could reach Sebastio.

Sebastio was in one of London's most exclusive hotels: The Chatsfield. Its darkness and exclusivity had enticed him. He had no desire to speak with anyone and sent off *stay away* vibes from his seat in the shadows at the corner of the bar.

His blood was still humming with an overload of adrenaline and arousal. He'd had to walk out of his apartment because one touch of Edie's mouth against his and he'd almost lost it.

He took a long drink of the whisky in front of him in the heavy crystal glass. He put it down with a clatter that made the barman look at him for a moment. Sebastio was oblivious.

The only thing that had stopped him from taking her there and then had been her audacious claim.

*I love you, Sebastio.*

Edie was lying. She had to be. How could she love him? She had played the long game and he'd been an utter fool. Blinded by her naive innocence and her fresh-faced beauty.

She was just angling for more. *Marriage.*

She'd left everything behind in Buenos Aires. Including the diamond necklace. The first piece of jewellery he'd actually picked out himself for a woman.

She'd left it all behind because she was intent on making him believe she was different. Genuine.

Sebastio noted the tremor in his hand as he lifted the glass again. When she'd held his hand over her heart and said that it belonged to him he'd felt a very weak part of himself crack for a moment... So he'd kissed her, in a bid to remind them both of the only thing there was between them. Desire.

He'd told her too much. He'd given her the key to strike right at the heart of him. She knew his weaknesses and vulnerabilities almost better than he did. And, exactly as his mother had done, and as his first lover had warned him women would do, she was intent on using that knowledge for her own gain.

So why didn't he feel better at that assertion? Why was it that all he could see in his mind's eye was the expression on her face just before he'd walked out... *Stricken.*

When Edie woke the next morning she felt groggy and disorientated. She'd slept for hours. But before she even left the bedroom she sensed the apartment was empty. She explored tentatively and everything was quiet. She didn't even know if Sebastio had come back last night.

Then she saw a piece of paper on the table in the main reception room and recognised the arrogant slash of his writing.

*Edie,*
*I have to go to Paris until tomorrow. In the meantime please think about where you want to live and I will set you up.*

*There will be no shortage of financial support throughout your pregnancy, and we will discuss what happens when the baby is born.*

*As for anything more, our relationship will not be about that. So please save yourself the effort of trying to convince me otherwise.*

*Call Matteo if you need anything. He's staying in the city for a few days and he knows the situation.*
*SR*

The note fell out of Edie's hand to the ground. It was as if he was afraid there'd been some ambiguity about his parting words yesterday. There certainly wasn't now. Maybe in the future some other woman would crack open his heart. But it wouldn't be her. No matter how much heat was between them.

*There was no hope.*

When Edie woke early the next morning it took her a second to realise she'd woken because she felt pain. Down low. Cramping. She got up and went into the bathroom and saw spotting.

Immediately she changed and went into the living room, searching for her phone. She was about to call Sebastio, without really thinking about it, but then she hesitated. First of all he wasn't in the country, and secondly she didn't imagine he would appreciate the interruption.

She had a sudden image of him lying amongst tangled sheets, his limbs entwined with those of some beautiful woman. The kind of woman whose cynicism matched his.

Another cramp pierced Edie's belly and she felt sweat break out on her brow. She remembered Sebastio mentioning Matteo and called him.

He answered immediately. 'Edie, is everything okay?'

'Hi, Matteo.' Her voice wobbled and she fought for control. 'I'm having pains and there's some blood. I'm scared.'

'Stay right there. I'll get help straight away.'

He terminated the connection and Edie sat on the couch, curling into a ball. She'd been so lucky in the last four years, but now all the fears about her health and the ghosts she'd thought she'd laid to rest came back.

She wasn't sure how long she'd been there, but it only felt like a nano-second when she heard the door and footsteps. Familiar footsteps. *Oh, no.* She looked up to see Sebastio in the doorway, looking a little wild.

She tried to get up. 'Sebastio—'

But he had crossed the room and lifted her into his arms before she could say anything more. They were out and in the elevator, and all Edie could do was study the hard line of his jaw and think to herself, *He's not in bed with another woman...maybe that's a good sign?*

Then she thought of something else. 'How are you here? I thought you were in Paris?'

'I was.' He was grim. 'I left early this morning—a change in plans.'

They were down in the basement and he was putting her into the passenger seat of a car she'd never seen before. He buckled her in and came around to the driver's seat, getting in.

Edie realised the significance of this. 'Where's Nick? Why are you driving?'

He was pulling out of the car park now, onto the quiet London streets. He said, 'He's off for the day, and a cab will take too long.'

Edie tried not to let the fact that he was driving for the first time since the accident get to her. 'How did you know?'

'Matteo rang me. I was on my way up to the apartment and the car that brought me home had already gone.' He glanced at her. 'Are you okay?'

'I hope so. There's a little bleeding, and cramps woke me up.'

Sebastio faced front again, his expression grimmer than ever. Edie couldn't help thinking that he must be cursing her for this new responsibility in his life.

Within minutes he was pulling in to the forecourt of an A&E department. Edie was whisked through to a bed and was being attended to and asked a million questions before she could even get her breath back.

She told the consultant about her cancer, and the treatment she'd received, and as she did so she was conscious of Sebastio's brooding presence in the corner. The consultant asked for her doctor's details and Edie gave them, knowing they'd need all her history.

For a few hours she was poked and prodded and asked yet more questions. Sebastio moved in and out of the room, speaking on his phone or just sitting or standing. All the time he was looking at Edie as if she might explode at any moment.

Later that afternoon the consultant came back in, looking weary but pleased. Edie held her breath.

The woman smiled. She said, 'Well, the fact that you

got pregnant is indeed good news, Edie. And you're very lucky—you know your chances were so slim as to be almost nil?'

'I know,' Edie said, not looking at Sebastio.

'It's quite miraculous, but it would appear that the radiation you underwent has not been as detrimental to your reproductive organs as feared.' She continued, 'I'm confident nothing is wrong. Spotting and cramping can be fairly common in early pregnancy. However, we'll keep you here for a few days' observation, just to make sure everthing is okay, considering your history.'

Edie felt a surge of relief. 'Thank you.'

The doctor left the room and Sebastio moved over to the bed. Edie forced herself to look at him. For a second there was something raw in his expression, but then he masked it. Her silly heart fell.

'Edie… I owe you an apology. I'm sorry I didn't believe you. If I had, then I would have insisted on you seeing a specialist and this wouldn't have happened.'

He looked tortured, and in spite of herself she felt her heart ache. She shook her head. 'This had nothing to do with you believing me or not believing me. Everything is fine. You do not get to blame yourself for this.'

The fact that Sebastio obviously acknowledged the baby was his felt almost irrelevant right now. Edie knew that the one thing she would not be able to deal with was Sebastio's pity. Because now he would have to admit that he might have been wrong about accusing her of manipulating their whole relationship, and then he would realise she'd meant it when she'd said she loved him…

She wouldn't be able to bear that.

She'd actually prefer his disdain and distrust. She was too vulnerable to take his pity on board.

He opened his mouth to speak but she said, 'No. I don't

want to hear it, Sebastio. Your note made things perfectly clear. We can discuss what happens next when I'm discharged. But until then I don't want to see you.'

Maybe by then she would have recovered her composure enough to discuss things without falling apart.

'Edie…'

She turned her face away and closed her eyes. 'I'm quite tired. I don't want to talk about it. Please, just go.'

For a long moment Sebastio stood there, but he knew it would be futile to try and talk to her now, no matter how much he wanted to. Or needed to.

He left the private room and stood at the window, seeing how Edie had curled up on her side, away from him. She was so slender, fragile. And yet he knew the core of steel within her now.

He had a flashback of her marching into his study in Richmond and saying, *'I want you to make love to me.'* The fiercely determined look on her face had been mixed with something much more vulnerable. And then he thought of how she'd so expertly called him out on his deeply embedded guilt complex. She'd known him better than he'd known himself.

He'd got it so wrong. And he'd started to realise that last night, in the middle of a glittering function in Paris. In the kind of milieu he'd avoided for so long by playing rugby, before tragedy and family legacy had forced him back into that world.

He'd seen a vision of himself in the future, still alone amongst the same social piranhas. Clinging on to his rigid beliefs. His toxic cynicism. The full enormity of the fact that Edie was pregnant with his child had hit him, finally sinking in, and an indescribable feeling of joy had bubbled up inside him, breaking apart the protective shell he'd worn for so long.

He'd changed his plans to come back to London as soon as possible, suddenly filled with a sense of dread that it might be too late. And then Matteo had called. And when Sebastio had seen Edie curled up on the couch looking so pale and vulnerable he'd almost lost it. She'd been far too reminiscent of another pregnant woman he hadn't been able to protect.

He hadn't been able to stop the insidious spreading of guilt, which had been compounded as the consultant had confirmed that of course Edie had been telling the truth about her cancer.

And then she'd cut him off. Told him to leave.

What had he expected? For a moment a sense of bleakness pervaded Sebastio as he looked at Edie's slight form under the bed covers. It couldn't be too late. Surely if she'd meant what she'd said…?

It was bitterly ironic, but for a man like Sebastio who had never admitted to feelings as wishy-washy as hope and optimism, suddenly they were the only things he had to cling to…

# CHAPTER TEN

WHEN EDIE WOKE again Matteo was in the room. And for the next few days Matteo was her constant companion. When she asked about Sebastio he just said something vague about him having returned to Argentina on business.

He wasn't even in the country. Edie felt acutely disappointed, in spite of her brave words to him to leave her alone.

When she was discharged with a clean bill of health it was Matteo who took her back to the apartment and who cared for her. She hadn't wanted to worry her parents, who were only just back from their cruise. Not after everything they'd been through before. She planned on going up to visit once she'd passed the three-month mark.

Sebastio rang intermittently, but their conversations were clipped and impersonal. He asked how she was and she said *fine*. He told her he would be in Argentina for another week or so and they would talk when he got back.

Edie dreaded the prospect as much as she welcomed it. But in the meantime, because she was going crazy, she was going to do everything she could to start feeling in control of her life again.

*A week later*

Sebastio stood across the street and took in the scene. Edie was in one of the main Marrotts windows, working on a new display. He was vaguely aware that it looked like a display for bed linen, complete with bedroom furniture. She was dressed much as he'd first seen her, in black trousers and a grey sleeveless top, a white shirt.

He felt like scowling, and vowed to burn everything monochrome in her wardrobe. But first... For the first time in his life he couldn't predict an outcome, and it made him feel uncharacteristically anxious.

And then he saw her drag a stepladder from the side and climb up it to reach something above her head. The spurt of irritation mixed with concern galvanised Sebastio across the road...

Edie was straining up to reach the hook in the ceiling through which she could feed the curtain, but it was just out of her reach. She bit back a curse and the very annoying prickle of frustrated tears. Her emotions were all over the place.

Matteo had officially marked his place as World's Sweetest Man Ever when he'd read from the pregnancy book he'd bought her and told her, 'It's entirely normal to be feeling up and down at this time. Your hormones are going haywire. And also—' he'd coughed and coloured a little '—your... er...breasts might be feeling a little tender.'

Edie might have laughed if she hadn't felt like crying. Again. Her breasts were tender. Achingly so. But she had a feeling that it had more to do with the fact that she craved Sebastio's touch than with anything to do with her pregnancy.

*And he won't be touching you again*, reminded a frigid voice.

Edie made one last attempt to reach the hook, just as a deep and infinitely memorable voice came from nearby.

'*Dios*, Edie. Get down from there!'

It all happened so fast it was a blur, but as she turned in shock she lost her precarious balance on the ladder and felt herself falling into thin air—only to be caught at the same moment in Sebastio's arms.

She landed against his chest with a little *oof.* And then it was so delicious being held in his arms that it took her a second of staring deep into those grey eyes before she remembered what was at stake and panicked.

'I'm fine—you can put me down.'

For a second Sebastio's arms tightened around her, but then he let her go, setting her back on her feet. She nearly regretted it because her legs were so wobbly.

Sebastio spoke first, a frown line between his eyes. 'What were you doing up a ladder?' He gestured with an arm. 'What are you even doing here? You are the mother of my child! You should be taking care of yourself.'

Shock and anger mixed together inside Edie. It was too much to see Sebastio here like this. A cruel kind of déjà-vu.

She put her hands on her hips. 'I was doing just fine until you scared the life out of me.' She clamped her mouth shut to stop anything else from tumbling out.

For the first time Edie noticed that he looked dishevelled and strained. He wore a suit, but no tie. The top button of his shirt was open. The suit was creased.

'Edie, we need to talk… Can we talk somewhere?'

She shook her head. She was afraid if she went somewhere with Sebastio the frail control on her emotions would unravel altogether. 'No, we can talk here—it's perfectly private.'

Both of them were oblivious to the small crowd gathering outside the window. And to the fact that Jimmy had just come to the doorway, taken one look at their faces and softly closed the door.

Sebastio started to pace in the small space, which was

dressed as a bedroom, complete with an artfully angled bed the better to display the luxurious linen.

He stopped and looked at her.

Edie blurted out, 'What are you doing here?'

He came close. Close enough for Edie to see that there was a light in his eyes that she had never seen before. It made her heart beat faster. It scared her. Because she couldn't foster any hope. He'd killed all hope.

'Sebastio…?'

He took her hands in his.

'When I saw the pregnancy test I felt totally betrayed. I believed the worst. I interpreted everything in the worst light. To me there wasn't even a possibility that you hadn't orchestrated it for your benefit. It confirmed all the tiny doubts I'd ever had about you. That you couldn't possibly be as innocent as you seemed. That you couldn't possibly be as open as you were. As you are.

'My whole life has directed me to a world view that supports my cynicism. My first lover warned me that people would only ever want me for my wealth and success. My parents' relationship was so toxic I vowed never to marry or have children, in case I inflicted the same pain on them…

'When the car crash happened, the reason I found it so hard to let go of the guilt wasn't just because I was driving, or because Victor blamed me. It was because I was deeply envious of what Maya and Victor had. Their love and happiness. I was so intent on reinforcing my cynicism in response to something Maya had said that I got distracted and took my eyes off the road for a split second. And in that moment we crashed.

'My cynical comment was the last thing Victor remembered. He knew that I was envious of what they had and in the aftermath it was easy for him to blame me…to hit me where it hurt. And I let him because I thought I deserved it. I felt ashamed.'

His hands tightened on hers. 'I know now that even if I hadn't been distracted I still wouldn't have been able to avoid that drunk driver.'

Edie's heart ached even as she tried desperately to protect herself. 'You don't have to explain all of this,' she said.

He shook his head. 'The reason I went back to Buenos Aires was because I wanted to come back to you and leave you in no doubt about what I'm saying. I've made my peace with Victor. You were right. He is happy again. We laid a lot of ghosts to rest, and that's something that I know wouldn't have happened if I hadn't met you.'

A warm glow infused Edie's chest. 'I'm sure it would have happened sooner or later.'

Sebastio grimaced. 'I doubt it. I needed someone to come along and break me apart so I could start to come back together again.'

Edie's heart spasmed. 'What are you talking about?'

He looked at her and she gulped. She'd never seen such intensity in his expression. Or she had… It had been that night in the shower, when he'd been so raw after the nightmare.

'I love you, Edie… I love you more than life itself. It just took me a while to figure that out, because you were right. How could I know what love was? Except I do know… I loved my grandmother and she loved me. For a long time I buried the memory of those feelings, though, too afraid that if I admitted to them I'd become weak. I had to be strong to weather my parents' disregard.'

Edie lifted a trembling hand to Sebastio's face. She couldn't speak.

'It wasn't until you came along that I started to allow myself to feel again. To trust again. To want more again.'

He cupped her cheek. 'It started that night in the club, four years ago. I saw you and I felt something break inside me. When you looked at me I felt exposed, as if you could see right into me to where I was so dark and jaded.'

Edie whispered, 'I felt it too…like you could see what I'd been through. How isolated I felt…out of place.'

He nodded. 'I also saw how young you were—and innocent. I didn't want to taint you with my cynicism.'

He took a deep breath. 'Edie, I want to ask…'

He stopped and looked endearingly uncertain. Then he got down on one knee in front of her.

Edie's jaw fell open. Her legs went so weak that they collapsed, and she found herself sitting on the edge of something soft. She didn't even know what.

He still had her hands in his and he let one go to take a box out of his jacket pocket. A small dark blue velvet box. He let her other hand go and opened it.

Edie looked down to see a ring. A ring with a teardrop diamond that looked very familiar, and two smaller diamonds either side. In a platinum setting.

Sebastio said, 'I had the diamond from the necklace set in the ring… It's the only piece of jewellery I've ever picked out for a woman before… I think that's when I suspected how much trouble I was in…'

Edie looked at Sebastio, her eyes filling with helpless tears. 'It's lovely…'

He took the ring out of the box and held her hand. 'Edie, will you please marry me and promise to spend the rest of your life with me? Because if you don't…' He went pale. 'I can't imagine my life without you in it. I want it all with you. A family. A home.'

Edie smiled tremulously. 'A dog?'

Sebastio smiled too, his eyes suspiciously bright. 'I'd really like a dog too… So will you? Marry me, Edie…?'

Edie couldn't hold back any longer. She launched herself at Sebastio and he tumbled back onto the very expensive oriental rug on the floor. Her arms were wrapped tight around his neck, her aching, tender breasts crushed against his chest. But she didn't care.

She kissed him because she thought she might die if she didn't. And when she pulled back she said breathlessly, 'Yes… Sebastio Rivas…yes, I'll marry you.'

Outside the window the crowd had swelled to about a hundred people. Phones were being pointed at the window and people were clapping and wiping tears from their eyes.

Sebastio's proposal to Edie went viral within minutes.

When Sebastio finally extricated himself enough to put the glittering ring on Edie's finger it made a very dull January day much brighter.

# EPILOGUE

*Two years later. Richmond, Christmas*

SEBASTIO STOOD AT the main front door and felt his chest swell so much with love that it almost hurt. Edie and their fifteen-month-old daughter, Rose—named after his grandmother—were putting the final touches to a somewhat squat-looking snowman near the bottom of the steps, and he observed them for a moment while they were unaware of his presence.

Edie wore no hat and her hair was piled messily on top of her head in a topknot, tendrils of dark auburn falling around her face. She'd finally let it grow again...

Rose took after both of them. She had dark hair and blue eyes. Lighter than her mother's. Sebastio had never felt so terrified as he had the morning her slippery little form had rushed out of Edie's body and into their lives, but in an instant the terror had been replaced with a welling of love so intense he'd almost combusted.

Every day the intensity of that emotion felled him. But what terrified him even more was the prospect that he wouldn't have known this if Edie hadn't come into his world and brought him back to life.

Behind him the house was decorated to the gills in preparation for Christmas in two days. Edie's parents were due to arrive at any minute.

The scent of the massive Christmas tree in the hall tickled Sebastio's nostrils and he had to smile at the thought of how comprehensively his life had changed. For the better.

He was back in the rugby arena too, working as a pundit for the big European tournaments, and it fed his soul to be part of that world again.

And Edie…

Pride filled him. Edie had started her own business as a creative consultant for event decorating. Jimmy was her business partner and Sebastio had become a frequent visitor to various houses and marquees, carrying Rose against his chest in a harness.

Rose spotted Sebastio in the doorway now and shrieked, clapping her hands. *'Dada! Dada!'*

Edie turned and looked up at him, smiling in that secret way she had that sent his body into meltdown. She'd been smiling at him more enigmatically for the past couple of days, actually, and it was begining to seriously unnerve him—as if she knew something he didn't.

He vowed to get it out of her later. But for now he pulled on his boots and a coat and went to join his wife and daughter. He counted his many blessings—not least of which was the chocolate Labrador that bounded around the corner and slammed into the snowman, showering them all with snow and causing Rose to squeal with delight…

And much later he did manage to get out of Edie the reason why she'd been smiling at him as if she had a secret.

Because she did…

The secret that they were to continue a happy tradition. Edie had conceived another Christmas baby…

\* \* \* \* \*

# COMING SOON!

We really hope you enjoyed reading this book. If you're looking for more romance, be sure to head to the shops when new books are available on

# Thursday 13th December

MILLS & BOON

# MILLS & BOON

## Coming next month

### THE SECRET KEPT FROM THE ITALIAN
Kate Hewitt

'Maisie.'

Antonio looked up at the sound of her name on another man's lips. The man was standing by the entrance to the hotel, a smile on his face as he held out his arms. Slowly Antonio turned and saw Maisie walking towards the man, a tremulous smile curving her lush lips, a baby nestled in her arms.

A baby.

Antonio stared as the man took the baby from her, cuddling the little bundle as he cooed down at it.

'Hey, sweetie.'

Jealousy fired through Antonio, although he couldn't even say why. So Maisie had moved on, found a boyfriend or husband, and had a baby pretty darn quick. That was fine. Of course it was. Except...

They'd spent the night together a year ago, and although Antonio wasn't an expert on babies by any means, the child nestled in the man's arms looked to be at least a few months old. Which meant...

Either Maisie had been pregnant when she'd slept with him, or had fallen pregnant immediately after. Or, he realised with a sickening rush, had become pregnant by him.

He hadn't used birth control. He'd been too drunk and emotional even to think of it at the time, and later he'd assumed Maisie must have been on the pill, since she hadn't seemed concerned. But now he remembered how she'd come to see him—how many weeks later? Two, three? She'd wanted to talk to him. She'd looked distraught. What if she'd been pregnant?

Why had he not considered such a possibility? Antonio retrained his shocked gaze on the man and baby, only to realise they'd already gone. Maisie had turned around and was walking back towards the ballroom, and presumably her waitressing duties. And his child might have just been hustled out of the door.

'Maisie.' His voice came out in a bark of command, and Maisie turned, her jade-green eyes widening as she caught sight of him. Then her face drained of colour, so quickly and dramatically that Antonio felt another rush of conviction. Why would she react like that if the child wasn't his?

'What are you doing here?' she asked in a low voice.

'I'm a guest at the dinner.'

'Yes, but…what do you want from me, Antonio?' She looked wretched, and more than once her gaze darted towards the doors and then back again.

'Let's talk in private.'

'You weren't so interested in doing that the last time we met,' Maisie snapped, summoning some spirit.

'Yes, I know, but things are different now.'

'They're different for me too.' She took a step backwards, her chin raised at a proud, determined angle. 'You didn't want to know me a year ago, Antonio, and now I don't want to know you. Doesn't feel very good, does it?' She gave a hollow laugh.

'This is not the time to be petty,' Antonio returned evenly. 'We need to talk.'

'No, we don't—'

'Maisie.' He cut her off, making her flinch. 'Is the baby mine?'

Continue reading
THE SECRET KEPT FROM THE ITALIAN
Kate Hewitt

*Available next month*
www.millsandboon.co.uk

# LET'S TALK
## Romance

For exclusive extracts, competitions
and special offers, find us online:

 facebook.com/millsandboon

 @millsandboonuk

 @millsandboon

Or get in touch on 0844 844 1351*

For all the latest titles coming soon, visit
millsandboon.co.uk/nextmonth